THE SECRET OF MARRACOTT DEEP

By
HENRY SLESAR

I0541433

ARMCHAIR FICTION
PO Box 4369, Medford, Oregon   97501-0168

CHAPTER ONE

Two days after he married her, Burt Holrood discovered that Jessie was half-wife, half-stranger.

The wedding had been a simple civil affair in the unromantic offices of a Los Angeles courthouse. But whatever romance the ceremony lacked was made up for by the honeymoon trip. The next afternoon, they boarded a DC-7 for Oahu in the Hawaiian Islands.

Jessie was all newlywed—sweet and bride-beautiful from the moment they entered the plane to the moment they pushed aside the latticed doors of their room in the modest little beach hotel called the Keehoa. But later that day, Jessie's mood mysteriously changed.

They were lying on the sand, glorying in the warm sun and fragrant air, when Jessie turned to Burt and said:

"Please, Burt. Would you mind leaving me for a while?"

His young, quizzical face, already showing a sprinkling of sun-inspired freckles, wrinkled with puzzlement. It was an engaging face, not handsome, but the kind you enjoyed watching. He said:

"I don't get you, honey."

"I just want to be alone for a while. I'm afraid I get that way sometimes, Burt. I just have to be alone."

He frowned, and then tried to smile. "Okay, Garbo. Mother told me there'd be days like this. but don't forget—it takes two to make a honeymoon."

She turned her face from him, her dark hair spilling over her sculptured shoulders. Jessie was beautiful in more than face and form. Her movements were beautiful, too, fluid and graceful like the movements of a dancer. But she wasn't a dancer; she was a semi-successful commercial artist, with her own studio in downtown Los Angeles. Burt was a photographer in the city, and they had met at a party for their allied trades. Within two months they had discovered enough about each other to marry. Now, as Burt watched her turn aside from him on the empty beach at Oahu, he wondered if he really knew enough.

He got up from the blanket and brushed sand from his knees.

"Okay, Jessie. I'll run back to the hotel and investigate the bar. Don't stay out too long."

She said nothing.

Burt stalked back towards the Hotel Keehoa with his spine stiff and his mouth grim. He tried to think of what he might have said or done to react upon Jessie this way, but nothing came to mind but the tender and passionate moments they had shared since the morning of the Wedding. It was a mystery, and Burt didn't like mysteries. He liked his life to be clear and uncomplicated.

The hotel, a sturdy four-story building of whitewashed concrete, was quiet. He went across the cool wood-paneled lobby towards the curtained doorway labeled BAR.

There was only one patron, sitting at a small wooden table near the window that faced the ocean. He looked up with a smile on his lined, British face that turned up one corner of his shabby gray moustache. Burt ordered a rum and soda from the Japanese barman, and sipped it glumly.

"Will you join me?"

The moustached man was grinning openly at him. Burt wasn't in the mood for company, but he picked up his drink and came to the table. When he sat down, the man said:

"My name's Nichols. Saw you arrive today, with your

MONSTERS FROM THE OCEAN FLOOR!

In the early days of our planet, the sea gave the Earth life in many varied forms; and through the centuries she has sustained and nourished mankind.

But for what past crimes committed by the human race did she now send a race of monsters from her deepest reaches? Monsters of unthinkable horror—many of them giant creatures, hell-bent on destruction. Monsters with dreams of world-wide domination…

The entire human race found itself on the brink of destruction in this bizarre thriller by one of the best authors from the golden age of science fiction, Henry Slesar.

FOR A COMPLETE SECOND NOVEL, TURN TO PAGE 71

CAST OF
CHARACTERS

BURT HOLROOD
*He was just your average newlywed with a beautiful new bride,
but his honeymoon turned into a vacation nightmare.*

JESSIE HOLROOD
*She was Burt's gorgeous wife and she seemed like the girl next
door, but her past was filled mystery.*

DR. NICHOLS
*He was an oceanographer, a doctor of science. What was his
unusual interest in Burt Holrood's new bride?*

ADMIRAL COLIHAN
*Getting this tough-minded Navy man to believe in the existence
of a race of sea people was going to be a tough sell.*

CROFTER
*The official record showed him to be a great deep-sea expert
and a loyal member of the Navy. Was he?*

KAMMER
*Before meeting this gentleman, Burt Holrood had never
previously known anyone who could breath underwater!*

wife."

"Yeah," Burt said. Then he flushed at his own bad manners and said: "Name's Holrood, from the States."

The man nodded. "You did not have to tell me that. And I suppose you don't have to guess that I'm British." He laughed. "Speech betrays most of us. Others things betray us, too, but one can be wrong. For instance, it was my first guess that you and your wife were newlyweds."

Burt looked into his drink.

"Now I'm not so sure," Nichols said. He looked out the window, towards the distant speck of Jessie's yellow bathing suit. "Unless you've quarreled, of course."

"We didn't quarrel," Burt said curtly. "My wife just likes to be alone sometimes."

"I beg your pardon." Nichols looked contrite. "I have an overdeveloped bump of curiosity. An offshoot of my profession. I'm an oceanographer."

"What's that?"

"Oh, just what it sounds like. My business is to be curious about the ocean; how deep, how hot or cold, all sorts of things."

Burt looked up at him. His face was angular and grave, his eyes serious, but his voice jocular. When he lifted his whiskey in his hand, he looked like a liquor model with ibis chiseled and weather-roughened features.

"Very interesting," he said dryly.

"You don't really think so. Your mind's on that beach. Well, I don't suppose I can blame you. Your wife's very beautiful."

"Yeah."

"How about another drink? My round."

They were starting on the third when they heard the scream.

Nichols' reaction was curious calm. He rose from his chair and looked placidly from the window. Burt joined him, and then realized that the scream had been his wife's.

"What's happened?"

The screams came again, short shrill outbursts of fear.

"It's Jessie!"

He exploded out of the bar, tipping over chairs in his anxiety. He ran through the lobby with Nichols after him, the older man running in measured but rapid strides.

Outside, Burt looked again towards the patch of yellow against the white sand and blue sky. But he saw another intruding color now, a splotch of bright red. He ran furiously over the soft sand, until he was close enough to the scene to see the source of Jessie's terror.

"My God!" he said.

His wife was trying to get to her feet, crawling away in loathing and horror from the monstrous crimson thing waving its terrible claws at her. Its eight spindly legs slipped on the sand, its feelers undulating rhythmically.

Burt recognized the ugly shape as that of a lobster, but his mind refused to accept the designation. No lobster had ever grown so gargantuan, or had such boiled-red color as this.

" Jessie!" he cried.

His shout seemed to thaw the icy paralysis in which she had been gripped. She scrambled to her feet and ran backwards into his arms. They watched the giant-shelled creature snap its claws viciously in the air, and then begin a slow retreat to the shoreline of the Oahu beach.

Just as Nichols reached their side, the red thing had entered the water, and its trembling antennae were disappearing beneath the waves.

Then Jessie began to cry.

She sobbed against her husband's shoulder for a full minute, while Nichols looked off at the horizon. When she was capable of speech, the first question she had to answer came from the Englishman.

"Mrs. Holrood—would you be willing to give me a detailed description of that thing?"

Burt looked at him angrily. "What the hell! Can't you see she's scared stiff?"

"Of course. You can take your time about it, but I'd appreciate a full description."

"I can give you one," Burt said tightly. "It was a gawd dam big lobster, biggest lobster you ever saw in your life. And red, like it hopped out of a boiling pot."

Jessie was murmuring against Burt's shoulder.

"Those awful claws…"

"Come on, honey." He steered her back towards the hotel. "This is what you get for wanting to be alone…"

"Mrs. Holrood," Nichols was persistent, "May I talk to you about this later? It's really very important."

"Later!" Burt said.

He guided her gently up the beach, feeling male and protective, and despite his wife's shaken condition, a lot happier than he had been ten minutes before.

Nichols just waited on the beach, watching them leave. His heel dug a hole in the soft white sand. Then he looked out towards the sea again, and his face was thoughtful.

Two hours later, Burt came down the squeaky hotel stairs, looking for the dining-room steward. He spotted the hotel manager, a small-eyed European named Ferner, and said:

"Mr. Ferner, is it possible to have dinner in the room tonight? My wife's not feeling too well."

The little man paddled his vest and grinned. "Ja, sure, Mr. Holrood. I understand." He giggled, indicating that he really didn't.

Burt was heading for the stairs again when he heard the dry, jocular voice of Nichols.

"Oh, Mr. Holrood. Can you spare a minute?"

He came over frowning. "Please make it short, Mr. Nichols. I don't want to leave Jessie alone too long. She's still pretty upset."

"I understand. Only I have to make one correction. The name is *Doctor* Nichols. Not a medical doctor. If I were, I'd be delighted to prescribe a sedative for your charming wife. But I'm only a doctor of science, ocean science, you see."

Burt tapped his foot impatiently.

"If your wife feels better this evening—"

"Look, Dr. Nichols, my wife is a delicate woman. That thing scared her half out of her wits. I'm having her stay in bed until morning. And even then I'd appreciate it if you didn't remind her of what happened."

Nichols sighed.

"Your privilege, of course. I don't want to spoil the honeymoon." His words were jovial, but his face still grave.

"Good night, Doc."

Burt turned on his heel and went up the stairs.

Jessie was dry-eyed when he reached the room. He sat on the bed and put his arms around her. Her response was warm and bride-like again, and he grinned happily.

"Feeling better?"

She nodded. "It was just the shock—"

"I can imagine. Boy, I knew lobsters grew big. But not that damn big."

She shuddered, and he held her tighter.

"Okay, we won't talk about it. I asked the manager to have dinner sent up here. I guess he thought we were mighty anxious to be alone. Come to think of it, he's right..."

CHAPTER TWO

The morning sunlight was bright between the slats of the blind, Burt looked over at his sleeping wife, grinned, and leaned over to kiss the inviting hollow at the base of her throat. He felt especially good this morning, and the thought of a pre-breakfast swim made him hurry into his trunks and beach robe.

It was only seven-thirty when he walked through the dining room. There was only one customer, a bird-faced woman in her late sixties, who was stabbing aggressively at a poached egg. She looked up disapprovingly at his costume. He saluted her with a wry grin, and went out the door to the beach.

The water was somewhat cooler than normal, yet still temperate enough to be comfortable. He swam out some thirty yards from the beach, and then floated around with his face tilted towards the early sun. The sky was a blue masterpiece, and the one white cloud overhead looked like a misplaced pillow. It was idyllic.

Burt slapped at his midriff, and imagined he felt soft flesh. The thought made him eager for exercise, and he plowed his way through the quiet waves with long hard strokes. Then he sucked in air, and dove beneath the surface to get a look at the famed undersea life of the Island.

The moody, breathtaking colors thrilled him. A flat striped fish brushed his chest, and he grabbed for it playfully. Then he saw a different kind of fish. The sight startled him at first, until he realized that it was the familiar breed called Man.

He needed air by now, so he paddled his way to the surface and gulped in a lung full. Then he dove once more to get a closer look at his neighbor. He spotted the flapping rubber fins and circular facemask, and realized he was sharing the morning's exercise with a skin diver, complete with portable oxygen equipment.

The diver seemed to have noticed him, too. He beckoned upwards at Burt, and they both rose to the surface.

"Good morning!"

The man treaded water, and lifted off his mask. It was Dr. Nichols.

"Morning," Burt said, trying to keep afloat. "That looks like fun."

"It isn't. It's work—"

He began swimming towards the beach, and Burt followed him. The younger man's towel and robe were some forty yards from the site, but Dr. Nichols handed him a rough-textured towel from his own gear. After they had dried off, they sat on the sand and Nichols handed Burt an English cigarette.

They smoked silently for a while. Then the oceanographer pointed to the sea and said:

"I thought I might find our lobster friend, but I guess he's back for the deeps."

"What kind of creature was that? I didn't know they even had lobsters in this part of the world."

"They don't really. There's a kind of second cousin to the rock lobster here, but that wasn't a specimen of anything in the book."

"It was a big one, all right. Maybe we should have tried to catch it."

Dr. Nichols looked at him. "It's worth a thousand dollars if you do."

"What?"

"I'm sure the American-British Oceanography Society would pay it for our friend. You see, it's not the first time he's been spotted."

"No fooling?"

"He was reported on Oahu about six months ago. But the funny thing is—he was also reported on Catalina Island a year and a half ago."

"Catalina? That's a lot of miles from here."

"That's right. Perhaps not as far as you think, however—not when you're crawling on the bottom of the sea."

Burt grinned, and flipped his cigarette butt towards the water. "That's pretty deep."

"Deeper than you probably know. It's almost six miles deep, in the Mindanao Trench in the Philippines, and perhaps deeper than that in the place they call Marracott Deep."

"But nothing could live down there. Like our lobster friend, I mean. The pressure must be terrific."

"No," Dr. Nichols said. "For a human, the pressure of less than a hundred pounds could kill. But you must remember that the pressure of our deep-sea creatures is the same within as without. There are many living things in the deep, more than we can possibly know about. The miracle of many of them is that they can rise towards other pressures nearer the surface, and still survive. Their air bladders adjust to the change if they move cautiously. As long as they don't 'fall' to the surface, they're all right."

"You mean that lobster came from the bottom of the ocean?"

"I don't know anything for certain. The bottom of the sea is still a mystery, but we're learning more and more about it all the time."

Burt looked thoughtful.

"I've got a theory," he said. "How about mutations?

Atomic mutations? Couldn't all those pacific atom tests have produced the thing?"

Nichols' face went blank.

"Possibly. Shall we start back for the hotel? I could eat a hen's yearly output this morning."

There was a pleasant surprise awaiting Burt on his return. Jessie was up and dressed and smiling radiantly, all ready for breakfast and a marvelous day. Her lovely shining eyes and good humor made Burt feel that life, as the soap operas say, could indeed be beautiful. He put his arms around her, but she shooed him off and told him to dress.

When they were seated in the dining room, Jessie began talking volubly, about every subject under the sun except the gallivanting lobster.

"I've just *got* to go back home with a tan," she said, her eyes dancing. "Can you imagine the wisecracks of the people in the studio if I come back all pale and white? You know what I mean."

"Sure, honey. Only take it easy; we've got three whole weeks to fry in. Don't do it all at once."

"Oh I'll be careful. Say, are you starting to tan, or just more freckles?"

He grinned. "Just freckles. If I can get enough of 'em, I'll look okay. Oh-oh."

Dr. Nichols was approaching their table.

"Good morning, Mrs. Holrood. Feeling better?"

"Just fine. Won't you join us?"

Burt introduced the doctor by his title, and hoped that he wouldn't mention the lobster again. But the Englishman seemed content to chat about the weather, the Islands, and the Hotel Keehoa's interesting assortment of guests."

"Now that chap over there," Nichols whispered humorously, "the one with the bullet head and bloodshot eyes.

He's been here a week and never leaves the water except to eat. Think he'd be waterlogged by now, wouldn't you? It's my theory that he's a Russian spy."

Jessie giggled, capturing the mood. But Burt sat silently, not sure that Nichols' humor was ever intentional.

"As for that old lady over there, the one with the newspaper, she never leaves the front porch. However, she makes it all up by playing a mean hand of gin rummy. Took me for six pounds last week; never batted an eye."

"And how about yourself, Doctor?" Jessie asked, a bit flirtatiously. "Are you the athletic type?"

"Not in the least. In case you've heard about my skin-diving, I want to assure you that it's work, not play. I hate water unless it's in a glass, and only then with a little Scotch in it."

Jessie laughed loudly.

"As a matter of fact," Burt said, "I've been thinking about the skin-diving business. Is it difficult, Doctor?"

"Well, you really should know what you're doing. However, if you'd like to learn, why not borrow my equipment this morning? I'm through paddling around for today."

"You mean it?"

"Certainly. Come up to my room and I'll give you a short course in the art. Join us, Mrs. Holrood?"

Jessie shook her head. "I like the surface, thanks. You run along, Burt. I'll go out for a swim meanwhile."

"Okay."

A few minutes later, Dr. Nichols was displaying the paraphernalia required in aquatic diving. His descriptions were brief and lucid, and within another hour, Burt felt prepared to brave a minor depth in the device.

"Now don't overdo it at first," Nichols cautioned, as they stood on the shore. "And don't try and reach Marracott

Deep on your first try. Just paddle around some fifteen or twenty yards from the shoreline, and get the feel of it. All right?"

Burt nodded, and slipped the mask over his face.

It was a strange and exciting experience, floating about in the dream-like atmosphere of undersea, not worrying about the need for air, having time to study and explore the exotic and wonderful marine life.

When he was under for some five minutes, Burt remembered Dr. Nichols' advice and decided to ignore it. He moved out further from the shore, towards the deeper water, where the sea bottom seemed to, slant sharply downwards.

Ten minutes later, he saw the movement of the red lobster.

It was hard to recognize the creature of yesterday in the hazy light. But as he came closer, the bright red color and enormous size was unmistakable. He pushed his way after it, keeping a safe distance from the great sharp claws.

It was heading for the shore.

Suddenly, the creature's speed increased. Its eight legs and huge claws began moving frantically, across, the ocean bottom, as if the need to reach the beach was urgent. Burt lost sight of it momentarily, and then decided to surface.

He splashed through the water and ripped off the facemask just in time to see the scarlet creature reach the white sand.

Jessie's scream was even more terrible than yesterday's, the horror compounded by this second appearance of the gargantuan lobster. He shouted to her and began swimming desperately to the site of the attack.

Then he heard the muffled crack of a rifle and realized that Jessie wasn't unprotected. Further up on the beach, his feet firmly planted in the soft sand, Dr. Nichols was aiming a high-powered weapon directly at the onrushing lobster. His aim appeared to be good; each repeated crack of the rifle reacted upon the creature. Most of the bullets seemed to be rebounding from its incredibly hard shell, but some were striking into the soft underbelly and brain.

By the time Burt reached dry land, the giant lobster was dead.

Nichols came towards them on the run, and Jessie fell trembling into Burt's arms.

"Well, we got the thing," Nichols said, "I wanted it alive, but this will have to do—"

"I like it better dead," Burt said grimly. Then his face hardened, and he looked at the doctor with inquiring eyes, searching for an answer. "What I don't get is this, Doc, the thing was after Jessie again. Twice in two, days."

"A coincidence."

"But it seemed to know where it was going. I was undersea at the time; I saw it heading for the beach—in a hell of a hurry. And there's a dozen people out on the shore now."

In his arms, his bride shivered.

Burt said:

"Why Jessie, Doc?"

CHAPTER THREE

The Hotel Keehoa came to sudden throbbing life. Guests that Burt had never known were there appeared in the lobby, buzzing about the improbable creature which had come up on the Oahu beach. A Hawaiian police official, summoned by the hotel manager, was busily taking notes that had no significance at all. As for Dr. Nichols, he was a blur of calculated activity. A phone call by the oceanographer commanded the immediate arrival of two burly young men, whose job it was to remove the carcass of the dead lobster and cart it to some place of study in Honolulu. Finally, the press seemed to get wind of the affair, and a grinning young Hawaiian named Hukoi was circulating among the hotel residents with a busy pencil.

When he approached Jessie, Burt threw up his usual protective block. But the little Hawaiian wasn't any less persistent than Dr. Nichols had been.

"Just a few little questions," he smiled. "Nothing to embarrass. For the local newspaper."

"Not right now, Mr. Hukoi. My wife's been too disturbed over the thing."

"Then perhaps you will answer some questions, Mister—"

"Holrood. Sure, I'll answer your questions. Just as soon as I get my wife upstairs."

Later, when Burt reentered the lobby, he found that Hukoi remembered the promise. He drew Burt aside, grinned amiably, and asked: "What is your wife's name, Mr. Holrood?"

"Jessica. We arrived here only yesterday, from Los Angeles. I'm a photographer, my wife's a commercial artist with a studio downtown." He went on to give a brief chronology of the events of the past two days. When he came to the second attack on Jessie, Hukoi's eyebrows lifted.

"Coincidence?"

"Of course," Burt said. "She was the only one on the beach yesterday, and today there were only a handful. That accounts for it."

"Naturally."

"Anything else?"

"One more thing." Hukoi lifted his pencil. "You have been married long?"

"No, just three days."

"Ah. And what was your wife's name before marriage?"

"I don't see why—"

"Please."

"Okay," Burt grumbled. "Her name was Jessica Burke. Can I go now?"

"Very sorry to have been a bother," Hukoi grinned.

Burt walked off, and saw the little hotel manager pacing the floor, squeezing his hands together in vexation.

"What's wrong, Mr. Ferner?"

"Ach! Such a thing to happen. A giant lobster in my hotel! But you understand, Mr. Holrood, the hotel is not liable for such happenings—"

"Don't worry; I wasn't thinking of suing. Where'd they take the creature?"

"Dr. Nichols is bringing it to the University in Honolulu."

"Great publicity," Burt smiled. "You'll have all the fishermen in town clamoring to get into the hotel now."

Ferner shrugged his shoulders, and Burt went to the stairway. In the room, he saw that Jessie was lying across the bed, face upwards, and peacefully asleep.

He tiptoed quietly towards her, and looked down at her

lovely, clear-planed face, more beautiful than ever in repose. He stared at her for a long while, until he began to sense that something was wrong. Her color was good, but there was something disturbing, something misplaced, something unnatural that he could not define.

Then he knew what it was.

His wife wasn't breathing.

"Jessie!" Burt cried.

He sat down on the bed and shook her by the shoulders. "Jessie! Jessie! Wake up!"

She stirred, and he could hear the normal rhythm of her breathing again. She opened her eyes, sleepily at first, and then in sudden panic.

"What's wrong? What is it?"

"Nothing," Burt said, sighing with relief. "For a moment, I was afraid—"

"Why? What happened?"

"You looked like you weren't breathing. I thought—"

"Don't be silly!" She leaned her head against his chest. "I'm just tired, that's all. I'm afraid you're not having much of a honeymoon…"

"I'm having a great honeymoon." He kissed her eyelids.

"I love you, Burt."

"I love you, Jessie."

It was a familiar dialogue, but they were fond of it.

That afternoon, in the lobby of the Hotel Keehoa, Burt ran into Dr. Nichols, looking flustered and busy. He stopped him in his tracks and said:

"Sorry to bother you, Doc. But I'm curious as to what's happening. Am I allowed to know?"

"Certainly, Mr. Holrood." He frowned at his watch. "I have to return to the University at five. That gives me a little time; how about a drink?"

"Sure thing."

They settled around the corner table near the window, and Nichols knocked back a sizeable amount of Scotch before beginning the conversation.

"It's the damndest thing," he said.

"What is? Our lobster friend?"

"A group of marine zoologists have been examining the creature for the past few hours. You should see the blighters are excited as kids with a new bicycle. Poking and prodding—"

"What'd they find out?"

"Well, it's a lobster, all right, no doubt of that. Some minor differences in the ratio of legs to torso—things like that. Also a superior hardness of the outer shell, proportional to its giant size. The color of the thing has them particularly fascinated. You know, at depths greater than about fifteen hundred feet, the fish are usually dark-hued, often quite black. However, there are often unusual exceptions. Prawns, for instance. They're often bright red, too. One of nature's pranks, I suppose, since all the red rays of light are gone from water at such depth. They probably appear just as black as the other fish."

"How do they account for the thing? For its size?"

"They have all sorts of tentative theories already—including your own atomic one, Mr. Holrood."

"Might as well make it Burt."

"Fine. My wretched first name's Percival, so I hope you'll call me Nick." He grinned wearily.

"Sure, Nick."

They had another drink.

Nichols said: "How's Mrs. Holrood?"

"Okay now. Been pretty rough for her, being attacked twice in two days. You can't blame me for thinking that beast was haunting her. But I guess you were right...coincidence."

"Poor girl. But I think you can enjoy the rest of your holiday in peace and quiet."

"I hope so. Like to try that skin-diving business some more, if it's all right with you."

"You're welcome to the gear anytime, Burt."

"Thanks, Nick."

Then the doctor fell silent, and his eyes became moody.

"Sure there isn't something else?" Burt asked. "You look worried."

"Not worried," Nichols said, "Just bothered."

"About what?"

"Something I didn't tell you—about the lobster. Something I hope you won't repeat to anyone."

Burt's brow wrinkled. "Sure, anything."

Nichols turned his glass in his hands. "We found something on the shell of the creature. We didn't notice it at first; perhaps we might have missed it entirely if the inspection hadn't been so painstaking. And it's something rather disturbing."

"What was it?"

"A number," Nichols said. "The number 42-361, stamped in black on its shell."

At four, after Dr. Nichols had departed for his appointment at the University. Jessie came down the stairs, looking rested.

Burt came to her and said: "Look, I've got an idea. Best thing for us is to get away from this place for a while. How about going into Honolulu for the evening? We can have dinner out, maybe dance a little, see the sights. Okay?"

"Fine," Jessie said. "I think that's a fine idea."

He captured the attention of Mr. Ferner, who listened to his request, and made arrangements for a taxi to take them into the city.

It was less than half an hour's ride into the famed capital of Hawaii, and they enjoyed the approach with all the innocent pleasure of tourists. Jessie loved the way the city rose from plains to mountains. She loved the encircling opalescent waters and the splashes of exotic vegetation. They moved close to each other as they drove through the main thoroughfares, as if the beauty of the city inspired them romantically.

The taxi-driver pointed out the local points of interest and pride: the spacious, flower-rich park, the clean high buildings, the territorial capitol, and then on to the splendor of the Royal Hawaiian Hotel that rose beside Waikiki Beach.

"It's so lovely," Jessie said. "Like a fairy tale city…"

"Notice something?" Burt grinned. "No billboards. Plain un-American, if you ask me. Put jokers like you and me out of business this way."

They rode on through streets bedecked with rare plants, with monkey-pods and banyans, umbrella trees, palms, bougainvillaea, tulip trees, and the ever-present hibiscus. The city was a garden, and in their present mood, it seemed to have been created especially for the Holroods.

They had dinner at the Royal Hawaiian, and dined on succulent native dishes that had them groaning happily at the end of the meal. Then they danced on the outdoor patio, until the moon rose fat and contented over the water. The setting was perfect.

By the end of the evening, all that had been lost between them since the hour of their wedding was recovered. Without tasting wine, they were drunk, and happily drunk, when they boarded the taxi for the return trip.

They reached the Hotel Keehoa close to midnight.

Just as they mounted the stairway to their room, Mr. Ferner, half-dozing at the front desk, called out to Burt.

"Mr. Holrood! A minute, please."

"What is it?"

"I'm very sorry," the proprietor said. "But the gentleman insisted, said it was very important—"

"What gentleman?"

"He's in the bar now. A Mr. Hukoi, from the Honolulu newspaper. He asked me to tell you to see him when you came in."

Burt frowned, and turned to Jessie.

"You go on up, honey. I'll take care of this guy."

"All right. Don't be long."

He let her go reluctantly, and went into the bar. His face showed his annoyance.

Hukoi was staring at a headless beer when Burt entered. The grin, that had seemed an inseparable part of the small, alert face, was gone.

"You have the time, Mr. Hukoi?"

The reporter looked surprised. "Twelve o'clock."

"A little late for an interview, no?"

"An interview is not quite what I came for, Mr. Holrood. I have information for you."

"What kind of information?"

"When I returned to my office today, I went to the morgue to get some background information on the lobster. I ran across this clipping."

He reached into his white jacket, and produced a folded strip of newsprint. Burt took it, his face puzzled.

It read:

REPORT: GIANT LOBSTER ATTACKS WOMAN

Santa Catalina, May 24: An enormous lobster-like creature has been reported on the beach of Catalina Island, California, by two witnesses. The giant crustacean, said to be bright red in color, is said to have

"attacked" a young woman as she sunbathed on the beach. The woman,
Miss Jessica Burke of Los Angeles, was said to have...

The print blurred before Burt's eyes.

"This is crazy!"

"Ah," Mr. Hukoi said.

"Look, buster, if this is some kind of a rigged-up joke—"

"I'm sorry, Mr. Holrood. I had no idea what I would find when I looked up the file. I was merely seeking to write a somewhat better story than your, er, interview afforded me. I didn't expect to find this interesting..."coincidence"...really I didn't."

Burt read the item again.

The woman, Miss Jessica Burke...

Attacked once by an outsized creature from the deep...attacked twice...but three times?

He handed Hukoi the clipping. "Thanks very much, Mr. Hukoi. It's very interesting."

"It does not disturb you?"

"Not in the least."

The grin reappeared on the reporter's face.

"Very well, then. Good night, Mr. Holrood!"

CHAPTER FOUR

The recuperative powers of the young are remarkable; within another week, Burt Holrood and his bride Jessie appeared to have no problems in the world.

Burt's friendship with Dr. Nichols deepened during the days that followed, although Jessie seemed to only half accept the oceanographer. The friendship centered upon their mutual interest in the art of skin-diving, and not a day passed without Burt improving his skill, utilizing the doctor's equipment.

On a Saturday morning, Burt made his first attempt at deeper waters. In a rented motorboat, he and Jessie explored the sea beyond the breakwaters of the island.

Burt tightened the flippers on his hands and feet, adjusted the portable oxygen equipment on his back, and grinned at her before slipping the mask over his face.

"I'll bring you back a goldfish," he said.

"Don't bother," Jessie laughed. "Just don't get mixed up with any mermaids."

He slipped over the side of the boat, and flipped his way towards the bottom.

The eerie light and mysterious quiet never failed to thrill him; the weirdly contorted plants and shells were like statuary in some castle of dreams.

Then he saw the man.

The sight of another skin-diver wasn't startling in itself; the waters of Hawaii were plentiful with them. But the cause of Burt's wonderment was the fact that this diver had none of the life-preserving equipment he himself carried. The man wore only bathing trunks, yet he seemed as much at home in the deep as the fish themselves.

Burt stayed out of sight behind a tangled growth of seaweed, watching the strange figure. He recognized the man finally: the baldheaded man with the Teutonic features who was a guest at the Hotel Keehoa, the one whom Dr. Nichols had described as a swimming fanatic. But the shock of recognition wasn't as great as the shock of the man's actions.

He was lying down on the sea bottom. He was resting.

Burt came closer, and the thought in his mind made no sense. But he could swear that the man was asleep!

He paddled still closer, and in the murky light saw the man's eyes fly open, as if he had detected Burt's approach even in the silence of the undersea.

They stared at each other.

Then, with a bound that was incredible in the cumbersome depth, the baldheaded man leaped towards his throat!

Burt was so startled by the attack that he was instantly carried off balance. He brought his arms up to ward off the plunging hands, but they closed around his windpipe. He tugged at the man's forearms; they had the hardness of steel, thickly muscled beneath the smooth flesh. He thrashed and kicked his feet in an effort to break away, but the man held fast.

Then the baldheaded man changed his plan of attack. He twisted Burt's arm into a half nelson, and began to reach for the oxygen equipment on Burt's back. Burt was helpless in his grip; in another moment he felt a change of pressure inside the facemask that terrified him, and filled him with thoughts of suffocating death.

Violently, he wriggled his body until he squirmed out of the bald man's grasp. His assailant's thick lips parted in a ghastly grin, but Burt was too preoccupied to wonder how a human could survive with an opened mouth underwater. He was fighting to control his breath, before the air inside his mask vanished.

He kicked his way towards the surface, and the baldheaded man reached out almost carelessly to imprison his ankles.

He awoke with the pounding of a thousand surfs in his eardrums.

He groaned and opened his eyes, and seemed to see underwater faces peering at him.

Then the images clarified, and he realized that the anxious faces belonged to Jessie and Dr. Nichols.

"What happened?"

"That's odd," Nichols grinned, "I would have sworn you were going to say where am I?"

"You got into trouble," Jessie said lightly, but her voice was strained. "Your oxygen tank went on the blink. Luckily, you came up right near the boat. I brought you in and Dr. Nichols gave you artificial respiration."

Burt looked around their hotel room. When he looked back at Nichols; his face was tense.

"It wasn't any accident, Doc. I was attacked down there."

"What?"

"I said attacked, by our bullet-headed friend, the one you said was a spy—"

"I was only joking—"

"I know that, but whatever he is, that guy is more fish than man. I came across him on the bottom. It sounds crazy, but I could swear the guy was—well, sleeping."

He heard Jessie draw a sharp breath.

"When he spotted me, he made for my throat. Then he cut off my oxygen. When I tried to make the surface, he pinned my ankles. I must have kicked like a million mules in order to get away—"

"That's fantastic," Nichols said. "Sure you didn't imagine it? The sea plays funny tricks on the eyes."

"I tell you I saw him!"

Nichols went to the telephone.

"Who're you calling?"

"The police," Nichols said. "I think they ought to ask our friend some questions."

"*No!*"

It was Jessie's voice.

They turned to her, and she put her face in her hands.

"I didn't want you to know," she said, her voice muffled. "I didn't want you to ever find out, Burt."

"Find out what?" He struggled to a sitting position. "I don't get you, Jessie."

"About me," she said. "About what I am."

Dr. Nichols cleared his throat. "Perhaps I'd better—"

"No, stay," Burt said. He got up and went unsteadily across the floor to his wife's side. "You're involved in something, Jessie. Something to do with this man. Is that true?"

She sobbed once, and put her head against his shoulder.

"I didn't tell you this," her husband said. "But my visitor last night was that Honolulu reporter. He found a clipping in the newspaper files, about the first red lobster report. It said that the woman who was attacked by the thing on Catalina was named Jessica Burke. You never told me that, Jessie."

"I couldn't. I wanted to forget it—"

Nichols was watching in fascination.

"Tell me now, honey. Tell me all about it."

He maneuvered her to the bed, and they sat down. She took her hands from her face and stared at the floor.

"I'm not human, Burt."

The stunned look on her husband's face caused her to

explode in tears.

"No, no, that's not true! I am human. I am! Just different, Burt, just different! But I *feel* the way you do, inside. Exactly the same way, Burt—you've got to believe me!"

"You're not making sense. Different how?"

"In here." She thudded her small fist against her bosom. A difference in here. My lungs. An air bladder…"

"What?"

Dr. Nichols' reaction was a gasp.

"It's true, Burt. Don't love me the less for it—please don't!"

"Honey, honey," he crooned, his arms around her. "I wouldn't care if you had fins. I love you…"

"Maybe you won't. When you hear the rest—"

"This is incredible," Nichols murmured. He took a step closer to her, his eyes wide with professional curiosity.

"I was born under the sea," Jessie said, her eyes moist and distant, "In the place you call Marracott Deep. We call it…Akumu. It's a city, an incredible city beneath the water. It sounds insane to me even now, but it's there. I've never seen it, but it's been there for centuries…"

Burt was shaking his head, rejecting the whole idea, trying to keep his life normal.

"It's true, Burt. There are thousands of us living below, our bodies adapted over generations to the pressure. We've lived in peace until now, Burt. But now, with the land-people probing into the very depths…Akumu is afraid. Terribly afraid!"

"I don't understand. Why are they afraid?"

"Afraid of the land-people. Afraid of investigation, of invasion. Afraid of your curiosity, your hostility, your greed, your thoughtlessness. Afraid of your weapons, your atomic bombs, your careless testing of nuclear power… The Akumus believe that once the land-people know of the presence of their city, nothing less would satisfy them but some kind of belligerent action, and that would change everything for them, Burt. Everything! Don't you see?"

"No." Burt turned his head aside. "I won't believe it, Jessie. This is some kind of nightmarish joke—"

"You must believe me, Burt. If you don't believe me, you can't help me. And they'll kill me…"

He stared at her. "Why? Why you?"

"Because I'm disloyal, Burt. Disloyal to their plan."

"What plan?"

She twisted the bedclothes in her hand.

"About a hundred years ago, since the first depth-sounding operations began, the elders of Akumu have been sending representatives to the land. From infancy, they bring us upwards slowly, allowing us to become adjusted to the pressure changes over many months, until we are enabled to survive in the topmost layers of the sea. Then we are brought to dry land. We're amphibious; we can live in air or water; the greatest problem is pressure. That was how I was brought here, Burt, at the age of three…"

"I can't believe it! You look—" He stopped.

"Like everyone else? I know. The differences are all internal. I've always dreaded the thought that I might need X-ray examination some day and then you'd know."

"But why have they done this?" Nichols asked eagerly. "Why send these representatives?"

"I can't tell you that," the girl said. "Please don't ask me to tell you that. It would be a betrayal."

"Is it something dangerous?" Burt asked. "Are they plotting in some way against the land-people?"

"Please, Burt! You must understand. Even though I knew Akumu only as an infant, I was raised as an Akumu child. My 'parents' on land were Akumus who had been brought up from Marracott Deep many years before. I loved them as my own mother and father, Burt. And they taught me to love Akumu, and to be loyal to Akumu…"

"But you're not, are you?" Burt stood up and looked down at his wife, "That's what all the trouble is about. You're not being loyal, and that's why they want to kill you. Those lobsters—why do they keep—"

"Yes," Nichols said. "What about the lobsters?"

"They're the beasts of our world, the domesticated animals. Some are trained to kill, and they are possessed of the instincts of a bloodhound. There are others, too, far more horrible than the red lobsters—" She shuddered.

"But what have you done, Jessie? Why are they after you?"

"Nothing. I've done nothing. But that in itself is disloyalty. I didn't do what I had been commanded from birth to do. The first time, at Catalina, that was only a warning. But now—"

"Yes?"

She looked up at him, with such tormented eyes that Burt felt close to tears himself.

"Now I married you, Burt. A land-human. And there couldn't be any greater disloyalty than that."

Her husband swore, and smacked his fist into his palm.

"Let me remind you," Dr. Nichols said. "About our baldheaded friend."

"He must be one of them!" Burt said. "That's why he tried to kill me, because I saw that he was more fish than man—" He stopped when he saw Jessie's hurt look.

"How many are there?" Nichols asked. "Akumus—on land?"

"I don't know. Hundreds, maybe thousands."

Dr. Nichols went to his knees, and touched the girl's hand

gently. "You've already demonstrated which side you're on, Mrs. Holrood. I think you should go all the way. If you love your husband, if you want to be—well, part of our branch of humanity, then you mustn't mistake loyalty for foolhardiness. You must tell us what this danger is, what the Akumus are planning to do."

"I can't!" Her voice was shrill. "Believe me, I can't! Everything in me tells me to keep silent—"

"But if they plot something that will harm you or your husband—"

"I don't care about the danger. Because it won't happen in our lifetime. Don't you understand what they plan won't happen to Burt and me—it may not happen for a hundred years!"

Burt said: "How do you know?"

"Because I know, because that's what the plan is. It won't effect us, Burt. We can be very happy together—"

"And what about your children?"

Burt looked at Dr. Nichols.

"I don't know," Jessie breathed. "I'm not sure we can have children." Her face grew cold. "But what am I talking about? After you've heard all this, Burt, you won't want me for your wife anymore, will you? So the question's—academic."

Burt sat on the edge of the bed, and put his head down almost to his knees.

"You must change your mind," Nichols said carefully. "You must, Mrs. Holrood. Whatever the personal considerations, you cannot allow a catastrophe to occur. It may be as harmful to your own people as to us. Don't forget—wars have a habit of killing friends and enemies alike."

"It won't be a war," Jessie said hollowly.

"Then what will it be?"

"It won't be a war," the girl repeated. "A war has two combatants. There'll be only one—and only one weapon."

"What weapon?"

"Water," Jessie said.

CHAPTER FIVE

Burt and Dr. Nichols confronted the hotel manager together, and he shrugged his narrow shoulders at their
question.

"I know nothing about the gentleman," he said. "Except
his name is Frederick Kammer, and he gives his address as
Los Angeles. But I have not seen Mr. Kammer all day."

"No." Nichols said dryly, "and I have a feeling you won't
see him for a long time."

Burt said: "Let's get a drink. I need one bad."

In the bar, Nichols opened the discussion with: "Your
wife has to talk, Burt. You know that, don't you?"

Burt nodded silently. "But I love her, Doc. No matter
what, I love her. And I couldn't do anything that would hurt
her."

"You don't have to hurt her. You just have to find out
what these—undersea people are planning. Perhaps it's not
as serious as she thinks, perhaps she's—"

"Wait a minute. You're not saying that Jessie's—"

"Crazy? No, Burt. The damnable thing is I *believe* your
wife's story. That giant tattooed lobster, that half-man, half-
fish— I'm afraid it all adds up too well, but we still don't
know if there's evil intent behind all this. The thing to do is
find out, and find out fast."

"But how?"

Nichols leaned back in his chair.

"You're her husband, Burt."

"But you heard what she said. She wants to live only for
today—she figures this damned catastrophe, whatever it is,

won't happen until we're dead and buried. How can I get her to talk?"

"Perhaps it needn't be completely voluntary."

"What do you mean?"

"Sodium pentathol," Nichols said, "I can arrange for getting the drug. But you'll have to arrange for its use, Burt."

"Truth serum?"

"Something like that. I know you won't like the idea, but you have to see the wisdom of it. It's as much for Jessie's own protection as ours. We've got to know what we're fighting before we can deal with it."

"I don't know." Burt gripped his glass.

"It's the only way I can think of. If you've got a better idea—"

"All right...I'll see what I can do."

They walked up the stairway to the first floor some ten minutes later, and parted at the door of the Holroods' hotel room.

" Jessie?" Burt said.

She wasn't in the room, but the door of the bath was open. He stepped over to it.

"Jessie, you all right?"

Then he saw her body crumpled on the floor, and the spreading red stain on her dress.

The small room was crowded in thirty seconds after Burt's shout of alarm. Dr. Nichols, Ferner, and a short-winded puffy-cheeked man who was the hotel doctor, all bustled around the girl, until the physician was able to turn to the anxious husband and say:

"She'll be all right. The cut wasn't very deep; she missed the main artery completely."

He bandaged the torn wrist, and then raised his eyebrows

at Burt.

"Accident, would you say? If it was a suicide attempt; then I'm obligated to report it, Mr. Holrood."

"Of course it was an accident," Nichols snapped. "I'm Dr. Percival Nichols of the American-British Oceanography Society; I'm a close friend of the Holroods. We were celebrating only a few minutes ago. Mrs. Holrood is definitely not the suicide type."

The doctor shrugged. "However, the wound was inflicted with a razor—'"

"It was an accident," Burt said. "I'll swear to that."

"Very well." He sighed, and reached for his instrument case. "She's still unconscious, but she'll be all right in an hour or so. Perhaps I should give her a sedative…"

Burt and Nichols exchanged glances.

"Yes," Nichols said, "a sedative would be a good idea. But if you don't mind, Doctor, I'd prefer to have my own physician administer it."

The doctor bristled. "Very well."

"No offense. Sort of an idiosyncrasy of mine."

"Naturally. Well, call me if I'm needed, Mr. Holrood. I'm always around."

Within an hour, the medical man summoned by Dr. Nichols to the Hotel Keehoa bustled into the room. He was a pale, gruff-looking man with a brusque manner.

"Damn foolishness if you ask me," he said to Nichols. "You have written permission to use this drug on the woman?"

"Her husband's permission, yes. But there's something important at stake, Dr. Hallam. I wouldn't have dragged you in from Honolulu if it wasn't vital."

The doctor grumbled some more, and then prepared the fluid in the hypodermic. Just before he inserted the needle, he said: "Hope you know what you're doing; I don't like any kind of shenanigan."

After a few moments, Dr. Nichols was questioning Jessie, who groaned and moved her head from side to side on the pillow. Burt looked on, feeling miserable.

"Mrs. Holrood…Jessie…can you hear me?"

"What…what is it?"

"I'd like you to tell us about Akumu, Jessie. I'd like you to tell us everything you know…"

"Akumu," she repeated, her face contorted.

"What is the plan, Jessie? What are they going to do?"

"Must keep them…keep them from finding out…our sacred duty…"

"What sacred duty, Jessie? Are you speaking of the Akumus now on land?"

"Yes," the girl said. "We must guard the secret closely, until the time for the great hour…"

Nichols looked at Burt. "That must be the task set for Jessie and the other Akumus on land—to prevent the land-people from discovering the city's existence, until they were ready to strike. But strike how?"

He bent over Jessie again.

"How, Mrs. Holrood? How will the Akumus complete their mission? Will they destroy the land-people?"

"Yes!" Jessie cried. "Yes!"

Nichols blanched. "How will they do it, Jessie? You must tell us how!"

"I can't!"

"You must…you can't help yourself, Jessie…you must tell us the whole story…"

"NO!"

She sat up, and her eyes flew open.

"Amazing," Dr. Hallam muttered. "Never saw an effect like that under narcosynthesis…"

Burt came to her, his arms comforting. "Jessie, please.

For your own sake, tell us the truth."

"I can't, I can't, I can't!"

She sobbed against his shoulder, and didn't stop until the room was cleared. Burt tried to comfort her.

Later, Dr. Nichols scratched his head and said:

"It's hard to understand. From what we know of the drug, she couldn't have resisted the way she did, unless there were physiological differences that might— Well, what's the difference. The point is we're still in darkness."

Dr. Hallam looked bewildered. "Is this a joke, Nick? Underwater people? That's an opium dream—"

"More than that, I'm afraid. We've seen a great deal of evidence already. But I think we need something else—an X-ray of Mrs. Holrood."

"No," Burt said stubbornly. "My wife's had enough rough treatment. I'm taking her back to the States in the morning."

"But you can't—"

"I don't care about anything but her, Doc. I'm sorry. But all I care about is Jessie!"

That night, he held her close and repeated his words.

"I don't care about Akumu. I don't care about all this talk of undersea people, Jessie. All I care about is you. I love you..."

"I love you, Burt."

"We won't ever talk about it again. We'll live our life and let the world take care of itself. Is it a bargain, Jessie?"

"It's a bargain."

But the compact was more easily sealed than maintained.

Four hours later, as the moon rose placidly over the calm waters of the Pacific, its rays slanting through the blind of their room, a sudden shadow appeared at the window.

Burt stirred in his bed, and pulled the light blanket over

his head.

The shadow deepened, and wavered.

He opened one eye and looked towards the window. The moonlight was suddenly eclipsed by darkness.

"What the hell," Burt murmured.

He pushed his feet over the side of the bed and sat up, watching the window.

Then the gray tentacle lashed through the glass, spraying the room with ten thousand shards, whipped its suckered flesh directly towards him!

Burt shouted with involuntary horror, and behind him, Jessie was jolted awake with a scream in her throat.

The hideous body of the gigantic devilfish filled the hotel room window, squeezing its soft flesh through the frame, its eight arms thrashing towards Burt. Instinctively, he reached out and grabbed a cane chair, raising it over his head and beating at the monster's hide. Jessie screamed again, and huddled into the corner of the room. When she saw the great tentacles close around her husband's body, she made a plaintive sound in her throat and collapsed in a merciful faint.

Burt struggled in the tenacious grip of the creature, almost overcome himself with revulsion as the cold wet flesh touched him. Wild thoughts raced through his mind, and a terrifying recollection of the poisonous secretion carried by the octopus. Its huge malign eyes and parrot-like beak filled him with something deeper than physical horror as the thing drew him closer and closer to its sac-shaped body. He began to scream uncontrollably.

Then blackness.

When he awoke, he smelled gunpowder in the room. He raised himself from the slippery floor, almost retched at the acrid sea-odor, and felt himself being lifted by a strong arm.

"It's all right," Dr. Nichols said. "We scared the thing off—"

The invasion was on—the pattern, carnage and destruction.

He looked up at the oceanographer, and his eyes filled with grateful tears. Nichols was holding his rifle by the barrel. There was no sign of the gigantic devilfish.

"Jessie—" he said.

"She's all right. Just fainted; best thing she could have done."

Behind them, they heard the frantic clucking of Mr. Ferner, the hotel manager. Nichols shouted at him: "Shut that door! We don't want the whole world in here!" He helped Burt back to the bed. "Fired two shots at the thing, but I only wounded it. It went off down the beach and into the sea."

Burt looked over at Jessie, lying across the bed. She was stirring now, moaning meaningless words. He bent over and touched her face, and her eyes opened. She flung herself at him, and sobbed wildly.

When she quieted, Nichols said:

"Mrs. Holrood, listen to me. You thought you could live with this secret of yours, but now you know you can't. They're out to kill Burt, too. You saw that tonight." She turned frightened eyes on him.

"You must give us all your loyalty. Your only chance now is to tell us everything."

"All right," Jessie whispered.

Nichols sighed deeply.

"I'll get us all a drink—and we can talk."

Later, sitting rigidly in an armchair, her face chalk-white, Jessie said:

"The Akumus plan to drown the earth, submerge it beneath the water. I don't know when it will happen, but I was told as, a child that it would be four generations hence. Their scientists are busy now, getting ready for the deluge. The only humans who will survive will be Akumus."

Nichols cursed under his breath. "Shades of Noah's Ark," he muttered. "And how do they plan to submerge the land?"

"I don't know for certain. But for the past fifty years they've been spreading equipment throughout the sea bottom, along the natural fissures that surround the planet at the core. I think they plan some kind of demolition around the globe, to cause enough tidal action to drown everything that lives by air alone…"

Burt slapped his knees. "It's crazy! We could never prove such a thing—"

"They've started experimenting already, on a small scale," Jessie said. "Causing minor earthquakes and tremors. You must have noticed it—a whole wave of earthquakes have been reported in the last two years. They're not from natural causes. It's the Akumus—getting everything ready…"

Her last words hung in the air, and seemed to chill the small room.

"What about the Akumus on land?" Nichols asked. "These so-called representatives. What's their function? When you were under narcosynthesis, you said something about them preventing the land-people from finding out about Akumu. How can they do this?"

"By infiltration. The Akumus have been specifically brought up and trained to work as ocean scientists—"

"What?" Nichols went white.

"It's true, Dr. Nichols. The only way the Akumus could prevent their discovery was by placing Akumus among the oceanographers themselves."

"That's fantastic! You mean my own colleagues?"

"I don't know how many, or who they are. But there can't be any doubt of it, Doctor. Many of your co-workers must be Akumus—"

The personal note in Jessie's revelation seemed to stun the doctor even more than the fantastic plan for drowning the continents. He sat down on the edge of the bed and stared at the floor, his hands kneading the bedcovers.

"What a terrible idea. My own people…even my friends…"

Jessie looked at her husband. "I had oceanography training too, Burt. I was supposed to enter the field when I completed school. But then, when my Akumu 'parents' were killed, I resisted the idea and became an artist."

"Killed? What killed your 'parents?'"

"I still don't know. Something awful—"

"One of those damned sea beasts?"

Her hands covered her face. "They were off on a motor trip; their bodies were found on the shore, horribly mangled. That's all I know."

"Were they disloyal, too?"

"I…I guess so. They never spoke much of Akumu after I grew up. They became so quiet and withdrawn. I think they had come to love the land, perhaps more than they loved their memory of Akumu…"

"Then maybe there are other disloyal ones," Burt said. "Maybe your own colleagues, Doctor—"

The doctor stood up.

"We can't afford to wait another day. I want you both to leave with me tomorrow for Washington."

"Why?"

"I have a close friend, in the Navy Department. Admiral Jake Colihan. I want him to hear every word of this. He's probably as skeptical a man as we'll run across there; he'll be a good test. Are you willing to come with me?"

Burt linked his arm with his wife's.

"We'll come."

CHAPTER SIX

The next day, the honeymooners and Dr. Percival Nichols boarded a plane stateside-bound. They made another connection in San Francisco, and went directly on to Washington, D. C. A long coded telegram, sent from Hawaii, preceded them to the capital. But despite the forewarning, the man they had come to see was too busy for a consultation until three days after their arrival.

When the meeting was finally arranged, they learned that Nichols had accurately described Vice-Admiral Jake Colihan's skeptical nature. He was a small, pocketsize naval officer, with an overlarge head and heavy-lidded eyes. While Dr. Nichols talked, he spun around slowly in the swivel chair behind his desk, frowning so hard that every crease in his sun-browned face seemed to deepen. At certain points, he asked short, crisp questions of Jessie. Her replies, delivered haltingly, caused him to grunt.

After an hour and a half of patient listening, he folded his fingers under his chin and said:

"Let's have the truth, Nick. What is it, some kind of publicity stunt for the Society?"

The doctor's face fell. Then he rallied, and with all the intensity his voice held repeated his belief in Jessie's story.

Still Admiral Colihan seemed unperturbed.

Then Nichols exploded. "Damn it, Jake! What the hell have they done to you? You used to be a cocky son-of-a-gun; now you look like a brass monkey behind that desk. Do you think I'd stick my neck out if I didn't believe all this?"

Colihan grunted. "Okay, Nick, don't raise your blood

pressure on my account. Least you can do is give me time to dig into the story. If there's something in it, I should find somebody to corroborate it."

"Maybe you won't. That's what's so bloody frustrating about this affair."

"Don't be so sure. I know at least one man who should know. Commander Hal Crofter, probably the shrewdest deep-sea man in the business, Navy-style. You know Hal?"

"Of course. But he may be as ignorant now as I was, three weeks ago."

"Well, let's give him a call," the Admiral said.

On the other side of the desk, Burt and Jessie sighed, hating the thought of rehashing the story once more.

But they did, for a sharp-featured Lieutenant Commander, who listened expressionlessly to the strange tale.

Then Crofter said: "Interesting, mighty interesting. I've had a few ideas about these mammoth sea-beasts myself. Got a file in my office, including a recent report on a giant squid and stingray that showed up in the Caribbean a month or so ago. I'm pretty certain that they're atomic mutations—"

"No!" Jessie said. "They were there long before the atom tests!"

Crofter smiled at her indulgently. "There? You mean this—undersea city you came from?"

"Yes. From Akumu."

"Of course." His voice was bland. "Well, I don't say it's impossible—"

"You don't believe us," Burt said tightly.

"I didn't say that. I've been an oceanographer for many years, Mr. Holrood. I believe I know a thing or two about the sea, and what might and might not be under it—"

Nichols was fuming by now.

"All right. Ignore the whole thing. Wait until there are

more earth tremors, wait until there are tidal waves! Wait until the whole bloody world goes under—"

Burt leaned forward.

"Commander Crofter…"

"Yes, Mr. Holrood?"

"Would you submit yourself to an X-ray examination?"

The question startled them all.

Crofter blinked, and then recovered his smile. "Certainly not. Why should I, Mr. Holrood?"

"You heard the story. I was just wondering if you would care to—well, exonerate yourself from any suspicion of prejudice in this matter."

Admiral Colihan's small face went crimson. "This is ridiculous, young man. Nick, I think you've carried this joke far enough."

The doctor sighed in surrender.

"All right, Jake. You're more hardheaded than ever. But that doesn't mean I'm going to stop trying. If you change your mind, you can reach us at the Hotel Broadmoor."

The Holroods and Dr. Nichols had adjoining rooms at the hotel. They returned there at five in the afternoon, and Nichols went off to keep an appointment. He left with one consolatory sentence directed at Jessie.

"You won't have to worry about sea monsters here…"

At six, Burt went into the lobby to get the evening paper. As he stood at the newsstand, the short hairs on the back of his neck began to tingle, and he couldn't erase the impression that he was being watched.

He surveyed the lobby casually. It was crowded with people, scurrying back and forth, sitting in the leather sofas and armchairs, chatting, reading newspapers, smoking quietly. None appeared to be interested in him.

He shrugged, and started back for the elevators.

There was a narrow mirror set between the cars, and it was only an accidental movement of his eyes that enabled him to see the man behind him.

With a shock, he realized that it was Kammer, the water-breathing guest from the Hotel Keehoa in Hawaii, the Akumu who had tried to drown him.

He caught the baldheaded man's eyes in the glass, and Kammer turned swiftly on his heel and walked to the exit.

Burt hurried after him, pushing his way through the crowd into the street.

Kammer was walking rapidly, without looking behind him. He walked in brisk, short-legged strides, and Burt had to double his pace to keep him in sight.

He followed him for three blocks, and saw the bald man turn into a side street. He waited for a moment at the corner, and then went after him.

It was an ambush, but Burt was expecting it. He ducked swiftly as Kammer's upraised fists descended towards the back of his neck. The blow glanced off Burt's shoulder, and he grunted in pain. Then he drove his own clenched fist deep into the man's stomach. Kammer went "oof!" and doubled over. Burt hit him again, throwing his body against the punch.

The struggle was over quickly. Once Burt saw he had the advantage, he bulled his way straight at the bald man, slamming him against the bricks of the building. He saw the man's naked head snap back suddenly and land with an unpleasant crunch against the wall.

Then he slipped down to the ground, senseless.

Breathing heavily, Burt lifted him up and dragged him towards the street. He was a short, thickset man, but his weight seemed all out of proportion.

A taxi came by slowly, and Burt waved his hand.

"Bars open early," the driver grinned.

"Too damned early," Burt grinned back. "Take my friend and me to the Hotel Broadmoor. Just down the street."

"Right, chief."

In front of the hotel, Burt put a five-dollar-bill in the cabby's fingers and said: "Give me a hand with my pal, will you? I'll never make it alone, and I promised his mother I'd take care of him."

"Yeah, sure," the driver laughed.

They struggled through the lobby with their unconscious burden, and Burt tried to ignore the disapproving and amused stares of the guests and hotel employees. When he got Kammer to the elevator, he steadied him against the wall and gave the operator his floor number.

Jessie came to the door and cried out when she saw Burt. He smiled weakly at her.

"I forgot the newspaper, but I brought something else."

She recoiled from the sight of the bald man, and when Burt dumped him ungracefully on the twin bed, she turned her head away squeamishly.

"We'll have to tie him up," her husband said, "Get me something, Jessie, anything. Rope, twine, maybe the cords from the blinds—"

"Shouldn't we call the police?"

"And charge him with what? No. We'll wait for Nick to come, and get his advice."

An hour later, with Kammer well trussed and gagged, and already stirring himself awake, Dr. Nichols arrived.

His advice was short and to the point.

"Keep him right here. I'll get that hardheaded Admiral over here in a hurry—even if I have to tear down the Pentagon. Then we'll prove our story's true."

He went to the telephone.

Admiral Jake Colihan looked down at the trussed body of the bald-headed man and his mouth opened.

"You've really gone out of your mind, Nick. This is plain criminal—"

"No," Nichols said. "The criminal part is still to come, Jake. This is the man who attacked Mr. Holrood in Hawaii. The fact that he followed us all the way to Washington is reason enough to believe he's up to something."

"That may be true, but—"

"Wait. The thing I want to prove is that the man isn't normal. If I had X-ray or fluoroscopic equipment here, I'd do it the easy way. But since I don't, I'm going to resort to something more drastic."

"What are you talking about?"

Nichols face went taut.

"We're going to drown him."

"*What?*"

Burt smiled. "Brilliant, Doc!"

"You heard me," Nichols said. "I'm going to dump our friend in a full bathtub of water. But you needn't worry about him; he'll be right at home."

"You can't involve me in this!" Colihan fumed. "I won't let you!"

"Give me a hand, Burt."

Colihan started a rush for the door, but Burt blocked his passage, snapping the lock.

"Let me out of here, young man!"

"Not until you've seen our demonstration."

"Don't make me use force," Nichols said. "I've got a rifle in my room, Jake. I'll turn the bloody thing on you if you don't cooperate. I'm serious!"

Colihan's shoulders drooped, and he smiled wryly.

"All right. You're either crazy—or telling the truth. Let's see your little demonstration."

With Burt's aid, the doctor carried the trussed figure of the bald man towards the bathroom. He was fully awake now, and he thrashed and kicked in an effort to get away. But they had the tub filled in five minutes, and were whipping off the gag.

"Help!" he shrieked. "Let me go!"

"Dump him," Nichols commanded.

They dropped him into the water with a splash, and held him down.

Admiral Colihan stood at the bathroom door, watching wide-eyed.

"You're killing him..."

"Not this way," Nichols said, panting with the exertion. "You can't kill him this way."

For ten minutes they held the struggling body beneath the water, his round eyes staring out at them with fury and loathing.

Still he lived.

Five minutes more were enough for the Admiral. He said: "All right! All right! Let him up!"

"Convinced now, Jake?"

"Maybe...but I want a medical exam—"

"Suits me fine!"

In the front room, they heard the ringing of the doorbell.

"I'll get it," Burt said.

He went in, his arms dripping with water. The bellhop outside the door looked at him curiously, and handed him the evening paper.

"You left this in the lobby, Mr. Holrood. All paid for." He was staring at Burt's wet clothing, mouth agape.

Burt dug into his trousers and produced a coin, then slammed the door behind him.

He was about to return to the bathroom when the boldness of the headline caught his eye. He raised it and read:

EARTHQUAKES ROCK
PHILIPPINES
HUNDREDS DIE

Nichols saw his face and said:

"What is it, Burt?"

"Look at the headline. Still more earthquakes in the Pacific, I have a feeling that Jessie's timetable is all wrong. I think our friends in Marracott Deep have decided not to wait a hundred years..."

CHAPTER SEVEN

It took twenty-five precious days of meetings and secret sessions and high-level conferences before a decision was reached. And even that day saw dissension among the military, political, and scientific brains that were assembled in Washington for a plan of action.

It was General Stafford, a youthful-eyed, trim-figured man in his late sixties, who chairmanned the meeting, and was most cantankerous about each proposal for meeting the menace of the undersea people.

"I say investigate further," he told them, "This body of evidence you've gathered is alarming, no doubt of that. But it doesn't constitute irrefutable proof."

"That's a problem, of course," Dr. Nichols said dryly, "At present, we have no way of sending an exploratory force down to the bottom of Marracott Deep. No deep-diving equipment can attain nearly that depth without being crushed like an egg-shell. The development of such equipment is not too many years off, but I'm afraid we don't have that much time."

General Stafford scowled at him.

"And you honestly believe that these recurring quakes are the beginning of this plot?"

"I'm convinced of it, General. They're following a pattern in the Pacific that leaves no doubt in my mind, or my colleagues, and they're occurring with increasing frequency and intensity. As you've probably heard, there was a number nine quake in the Hawaiian Islands yesterday evening, at dreadful cost of life and property."

Burt Holrood, sitting in a chair by the wall and feeling misplaced in this high-powered conclave, folded his arms against his chest and thought harsh thoughts about the General. Burt had been a corporal not many years before.

"And these sea-monsters of yours?" Stafford said, "You're certain they're part of this undersea city?"

"There's no other explanation. Only two have been actually captured—a gigantic lobster and octopus. The octopus was washed ashore only two weeks ago, on Brooks Island. We know it was the same creature that attacked Mr. Holrood and his wife that night in Oahu; my own rifle bullets were found in its body. I trust you've all seen the photographs which clearly show the identification number tattooed on its head."

"Incredible," a scientist murmured. "Branded sea--cattle…"

"And branded killers, too."

General Stafford shifted in his chair.

"All right, then, let's hear about this—counterattack you're planning."

The faces around the table looked towards the white--haired gentleman at the end whose aged but cheerful face looked up and broke into a wan smile.

"Dr. Uribe, of the Atomic Energy Commission," Nichols said, "knows the plan better than any of us. I'll let him tell you."

The scientist cleared his throat.

"I needn't tell this group of the exploratory work done during the recent International Geophysical year, with surveys Norpac and Equapac; nor of the work done in the last few years by AEC in conjunction with the American-British Oceanography Society. Basically, our purpose was to evaluate the age of the deepwater in the ocean, to determine how great the danger of nuclear-waste pollution.

"We had no such problem as this in mind, of course. But our findings may well provide us with the answer we seek here. We have established that the rate of movement and transport of the subsurface and deepwater masses are incredibly slow processes, and that the age of the water in such a place as Marracott Deep may well be over ten thousand years."

The General tapped the desk impatiently. "What does that prove, Dr. Uribe? As far as this counter-action is concerned?"

"If this problem is truly serious—and I'm inclined on the evidence to believe the human race has never been more endangered—then we would be justified by using Marracott Deep as a resting place for our radioactive waste materials."

The reaction around the table was excited, and somewhat fearful.

"We believe that by dumping such substances into the Deep, we will effectively destroy all life—of whatever kind—without seriously endangering the welfare of the rest of the world. There will be problems, of course, with fisheries and so forth, and probably some radiation troubles developing in the nearest land points to the Deep, but we can be prepared there, too."

He looked around the room solemnly.

"It is not easy for me to sit here and propose such a monstrous idea as this."

He bent his old head towards the table.

"I have nine grandchildren," he said, "None of them swims especially well."

There was silence in the room for a full minute.

Then Burt cleared his throat and said:

"I don't have any right to make suggestions. I'm only here out of sufferance. But I'd like to say something."

General Stafford nodded at him.

"There's one topic we haven't discussed in this meeting, but we should. I'm talking about the fifth column of Akumus who are on shore now, who have been infiltrated into positions of importance in ocean. I think we'd better find out who they are, and quickly;"

Nichols looked at the chairman sadly.

"I'm afraid that's true. We must begin immediate X-ray examinations of all personnel connected with oceanography in any way. We mustn't allow our counter-action to be thwarted within our own ranks."

"And what," Stafford said, "do you plan to do with the - Akumus you locate?"

"I suggest that the government place these men under temporary arrest, until their loyalty or disloyalty can be proved. Or until there is no more menace in Marracott Deep…"

When the meeting was over, all the hesitation and in-decision and arguments seemed over, too. It was a time for swift and methodical action.

A dozen different government agencies set their wheels into motion, from the Federal Bureau of Investigation to the Bureau of Naval Sciences. With speed and precision, arrangements to implement every part of the project known officially as "Anti-A."

Burt found himself an important figure in government circles, acting as spokesman for his wife and as special assistant to Dr. Percival Nichols. He attended meetings with some of the nation's top oceanographers, and listened to their analysis of the plan which the Akumus were already putting into deed.

"This map will make it clearer," a scientist named Vidor told him, poking his finger at a sectional drawing of the earth's profile, "This land area represents the surface of San Francisco, perched over the crack known as the San Andreas Fault. The fault is a break in the granite layer beneath the earth's crust, and at intervals it shifts and slides, causing tremors. If this process were aided along by some undersea influence—the results could be disastrous.

"Here, off the bottom of northern California, is what we call the Mendocino Escarpment, an immense fracture in the earth's crust more than a thousand miles long. This is one of several fractures extending from the San Andreas Fault.

"There is an extension of the California fault system in the Aleutians. You recall the earthquakes in the Aleutians back a few years? They give us a foretaste of what will happen if such quakes become widespread. The tremors in the Aleutians caused tidal waves as high as thirty-two feet in the Hawaiian Islands. The shock carries great tidal waves in concentric circles from the center of the quake. The recent Philippine earthquakes caused tidal action as far as Japan and Korea."

Burt examined the charts grimly

"Then enough earthquakes, of enough intensity, could drown the coastal areas—"

"Worse than that. If these undersea people have demolition equipment which can use the faults in the earth's crust to their own advantage—they can drown the whole world."

Dr. Nichols looked at the map and said:

"We'll stop them first."

Then the X-ray tests began.

Within four weeks, six hundred and forty civilian oceanographers, with some natural reluctance, paraded in front of the nation's X-ray technicians. A hundred and twelve revealed an unusual formation where their lungs should have been. The majority of these, faced with the photographic evidence, confessed to their origin at the bottom of Marracott Deep. Some protested their innocence to the last, but were placed under arrest and herded off to a special internment camp in Oregon.

Burt marveled at the discreetness with which the examinations were held. Not a word of the arrests leaked to the newspapers or public; no comment about Project Anti-A appeared anywhere in the nation's press. And more importantly, not a mention was made of the vital task imposed upon the aircraft carrier *Dragonfly* that was being outfitted in San Francisco for an unusual tour of duty.

Burt, Jessie, and Dr. Nichols visited the dock where the flying airfield was being readied.

"Look at the size of her!" Burt whistled.

"Biggest carrier built since the war," Nichols told them. "Large enough to carry a whole armada of jet fighters anywhere in the seven seas. Only she won't be carrying jets this trip. She'll have a lot more deadly cargo—"

"How will the crew be protected against the radiation from the waste materials? With all that hot stuff aboard—

"Everything will be lead-lined, of course. But not even lead shielding can hold back all the rays indefinitely. When they strike bottom at Marracott Deep, they'll be timed to release enough radiation to wipe out everything alive down there…"

Jessie shivered.

"I hate to think about it. They're still my own people…perhaps my own family…"

"I understand," Nichols said gently.

They started back for the parked auto some forty yards from the dock. There were two men in civilian clothes waiting by the auto door. One of them took out his wallet and flipped it towards the oceanographer.

"Dr. Percival Nichols?"

"Yes?"

"I'm sorry. We have to ask you to come with us."

He stared at them. "Is there anything wrong? Did something happen?"

"We're placing you under arrest, Dr. Nichols."

Jessie gasped.

"I don't understand you," the doctor said calmly. "Just what charge are you making."

The second man said: "You should know that, Dr. Nichols. You took your X-ray test this morning."

He looked at them with bewildered eyes, and then turned to Jessie and Burt as if to reassure himself that the world was normal. Then he smiled unconvincingly and said:

"There's some silly mistake. I'm no Akumu."

"We have our orders, sir."

"But it can't be true! My parents were—" He stopped, and seemed to grow dizzy for a moment. Burt put out his arm to support him. "I don't know who my parents were," he whispered, "I was adopted, as a foundling…as an infant…"

"We really have to go now, Doctor."

"We'll come with you," Burt said. "We'll follow in our car, Nick. I'm sure it's all a mistake—"

"Yes," the doctor said blankly. "It has to be…"

They watched the men lead him away, his steps hesitant and uncertain.

Two days later, Burt and Jessie were summoned to the offices of Vice-Admiral Jake Colihan in the Pentagon. They were relieved to see Dr. Nichols sitting unguarded at the Admiral's desk, but he no longer appeared to be the self-assured, vigorous man they had known.

Colihan leaned back.

"This is an unfortunate situation. The two people most closely involved with this affair—yourself, Mrs. Holrood, and my good friend, Nick—are members of the amphibious race we plan to destroy."

Jessie looked at the doctor, who met her eyes sadly.

"Dr. Nichols, unfortunately, knew nothing about his origin. Or perhaps I should say fortunately. His adoptive parents developed in him a love of the sea and its mysteries, but never once spoke of Akumu. It would seem that they, like yourself, Mrs. Holrood, wanted to live in peace on land. The discovery, as you can imagine, has been a shock to Dr. Nichols—and given us a tactical problem."

Then his face seemed to lighten.

"However, we have talked this over carefully at the highest level. None of us doubts for a second the loyalty of you both."

Burt sighed, but Jessie and the doctor just looked at the floor.

"The hard part comes next," Colihan said. "The destruction of your own people. The death by radiation of thousands of Akumus like yourselves. That is what we plan next week, with the departure of the *Dragonfly* for Marracott Deep.

"This isn't an easy thing for either of you to face, but nevertheless, I'm going to ask all three of you whether you wish the dubious privilege of making the voyage with the carrier."

"No," Burt said. "Not Jessie—"

"There's no necessity, of course. I just thought—"

"Wait a minute." Jessie's head tilted. "I do want the privilege, Admiral. I feel I should be there, at the end as at the beginning. If your regulations will permit it, I would very much want to go."

Nichols spoke, his voice tired.

"You know how I feel, Jake."

"Then it's settled. We weigh anchor on Thursday of this week. We'll make our rendezvous with the escort cruiser on Saturday. We'll be on the target area on Wednesday next."

CHAPTER EIGHT

The day broke bright and clear over the Pacific when the *Dragonfly* and its escort reached the point in the ocean over the place known as Marracott Deep.

Few of the hundreds of crew members aboard knew the real purpose of the carrier's visit to mid-ocean. Essentially, it was a dumping expedition, a gigantic garbage-disposal job, getting rid of tons of radioactive waste materials produced by the atom factories of the U. S. and Great Britain. Among themselves, the officers and men joked about it.

But in the Captain's quarters, and in the wardroom where Admiral Jake Colihan and his senior officers met to plan every step of the undertaking, there was no levity.

And on the deck, overlooking the incredibly long stretch of carefully-secured lead containers that lined the enormous surface of the carrier, Burt Holrood and his wife Jessie were also in a solemn mood.

"We shouldn't have come," Burt said. "There wasn't any need to come, Jessie."

"I wanted to, Burt. It would have been worse for me on shore, waiting." She turned suddenly fearful eyes on him. "Oh, Burt, what if it doesn't work? What if the radiation doesn't destroy Akumu?"

"It'll work. Nothing will be able to survive. All those giant undersea things, all the fish for miles around, all the humans that live down there..." He pulled her to him. "Thank God they sent you to the surface, Jessie. Thank God for that..."

She clung to him, "I wish it were over, Burt..."

But it wasn't over.

Half an hour later, forty minutes before the dumping of the atomic waste was scheduled, Burt and his wife met Dr. Nichols in the forecastle.

He greeted them with forced cheerfulness. "Another few minutes, and the job will be done. The Admiral's calling all officers into the wardroom for a final briefing. Let's go below and sit in."

They went down a series of tortuously winding ladders, until they came to the small meeting room. It was filled with high-ranking naval personnel, and four civilian scientists. Only one officer wasn't in attendance.

When Colihan walked in, he frowned at his audience and commented on the absentee.

"Where's Crofter?" he said. "I thought I saw him on deck."

"Crofter!" Burt said to his wife, "He's the guy we met in Washington—the Navy oceanographer. The one who thought we were having pipe dreams—"

The door opened, and the lean figure of the Lieutenant--Commander entered. His sharp-featured face was flushed, and he grinned at the assemblage.

"Come on, come on," Colihan said impatiently.

"No hurry, Admiral," Crofter grinned back. The insolence in his voice jarred the others, "No hurry at all."

"What are you talking about?" Colihan's small face was hardening. "You forget yourself."

"No, Admiral. I remember myself. I remember myself very well."

Now they were all staring at him.

"Something's wrong," Burt whispered.

Crofter stepped in front of the Admiral and raised his hands.

"I'll address my remarks to you all, so that everyone has a clear idea of what's happening—"

"Sit down!" Colihan thundered. "That's an order!"

"Orders be damned. You'd better listen and listen carefully, Commander, or when the bomb hits, you'll be a very surprised man."

Nichols jumped to his feet.

"What bomb? What are you talking about?"

"Ah, Dr. Nichols," He grinned at the scientist. "My dear colleague, my dear Akumu…"

"You're drunk!" Colihan snapped, "Place this man under arrest—"

The officers in the room moved towards him uncertainly. There was something authoritative about Crofter now that had nothing to do with rank.

"You really must listen," he said easily. "If you wish to save your lives, you must pay attention. *The radioactive substances must not be dropped.* The ship must be turned about and taken to San Francisco immediately. The atomic waste can be disposed of in any manner you wish. But it must not be dropped in Marracott Deep."

"Akumu…" Burt said quietly. "He is one—"

"Of course." Crofter looked in his direction. "Just as your lovely wife is Akumu, Mr. Holrood. Only I'm not a turncoat Akumu—I'm happy to be loyal to my home water…to do what I can for it."

"The man's mad," Colihan said. "Arrest him at once; we have work to do—"

"Wait," Nichols said. "Hear him out."

"Thank you, Akumu," Crofter bowed. "It's a wise decision. But I'm here to tell you that the moment the first lead container is dropped over the side of this carrier—the *Dragonfly* will be destroyed."

The room was filled with shouts of anger and disbelief and fear.

"It's the deadly truth. There are Akumus waiting below this ship, ready to explode a nuclear weapon at the first signal. That signal is the splash of the first lead container into the sea. If you wish to avoid this tragedy, I suggest you give orders now to turn this ship homewards."

"It's a damned lie!" Colihan shouted. "A trick! You would dare to blow up the *Dragonfly*—that would be certain death for you and everyone down there. The radiation waste would descend just the same—"

"That is the situation, Admiral. If you wish to sacrifice the life of your officers and men to prove that I'm not bluffing—you're welcome to go ahead."

"Jake," Nichols said uneasily. "Think this over—"

Colihan whirled on him. "You expect me to take advice from you?"

The words hit Dr. Nichols like a blow. His friend looked instantly contrite, and then his shoulders slumped wearily.

"There's no proof. It's all a bluff..."

"It's no bluff," Crofter said, "Look out the porthole, Admiral. You'll realize I'm telling the truth."

Colihan strode across the small room and peered out of the tiny round glass in the hull. He gasped, and Nichols and Burt came to his side.

The waters of the Pacific were no longer unruffled and unbroken blue. There were visitors encircling the giant aircraft carrier, hundreds of naked swimmers bobbing in the sea, dozens of strange aquatic creatures rising from the surface, giant squids and stingrays and jellyfish, and an enormous octopus with tentacles almost thirty feet in length, clinging to the side of the hull with its disc-shaped suckers.

Admiral Colihan stared at this fantastic encirclement, and every muscle in his small face seemed to jerk.

"What can we do?" he said, only to himself.

"We must have time," Nichols said, "Time to think it over!"

"It will be nightfall in three hours," Crofter snapped. "I'll give you until then."

He turned and stalked out of the wardroom.

When he was gone, Colihan cleared the room of everyone but his senior officers.

Burt took Jessie's arm and led her back to their quarters. She appeared white and faint after Crofter's announcement, and asked to lie down.

"Sure, honey. I'm going to try and find Nichols—see what he says about all this."

He went out, but Nichols was nowhere in sight.

For two hours, the Admiral and the ship's officers argued, but found themselves at a stalemate.

Admiral Colihan stood adamantly by his proposal to scuttle the carrier, but the others seemed solidly lined up against him. It wasn't a question of courage or sacrifice, they said, it was only common sense. There would be other opportunities; they would be better prepared next time—

"Perhaps there won't be a next time," Colihan said blackly. "Perhaps they're planning to make their moves now, right now…"

With half an hour left, and with darkness settling around the great ship, the decision was yet to be made.

Burt returned below and went to the wardroom. His knock gained him admittance.

"All decided?" he asked.

The officers looked at him wearily.

"I've been looking for Dr. Nichols. I couldn't find him on deck, so I—"

He stopped when he felt someone behind him. He turned and looked into the grinning face of Lieutenant-Commander Crofter.

"Only a few minutes left, gentlemen. I hope you've reached your decision. My friends in the sea are getting anxious."

The Admiral growled at him, "There's still time, Crofter. Don't rush us."

"Of course. But you must know by now that you have no alternative. The carrier must turn back; it's the only sensible course."

A communications light flashed in the wardroom. An officer picked it up, and then turned to the Admiral.

"It's the radio room, sir, message from the cruiser."

"Probably want to know what's delaying us—"

"No, sir. It seems that the message is for Mr. Holrood."

Burt blinked at him, "Me?"

"Yes, sir. They say it's very important."

Crofter grinned at him. "I haven't seen your beautiful wife around, Holrood. You must be grateful to Akumu for producing such a lovely woman."

Burt frowned, and pushed past him, heading for the radio section.

The operator looked up, his face puzzled.

"I must be crazy. But I could swear I heard that guy say your *wife* wants to talk to you—"

"My wife? You are crazy. My wife's asleep in her quarters for the past couple of hours. I left her there and told her not to leave—"

He sat down, and the operator pulled a switch on the board.

"Burt...Burt..."

"*Jessie!*" The sound of her faint voice on the wireless sent the blood rushing to his head. "Jessie, for God's sake! How the hell did you get on the cruiser?"

"Burt, listen—"

There was a crackle in the equipment, and the operator spun a dial, his eyes wide and curious.

"What's happened, Jessie? How did you get off the ship? This doesn't make any sense—"

"We swam," his wife said, "Dr. Nichols—" She seemed to be gasping for breath, "It was the safest thing—we couldn't return to the ship—they suspected us—"

"I don't understand—" Burt's voice was wild. "Why did you leave? What for? And where's Nick?"

"He wanted to come with me—he thought it was only right when I told him what I wanted to do— Oh, Burt, he's dead! I—I tried to bring him in, but he couldn't make it...his bad heart—"

"Jessie, take it slow!"

"I wanted to find out—to go beneath the ship and see if what Crofter said was true—to talk with the Akumus."

"Oh, my God..." he moaned.

"It was the only thing I could think of, Burt! I felt so—responsible for all this."

"But what happened?"

"We...we slipped over the side of the carrier into the sea...we went below...they didn't suspect anything at first...they thought we were part of the Akumu task force...there were even other women in the water."

She stopped, fighting for control of her voice.

Then: "I—I spoke to one of them...it was so hard...it was a language I hadn't had on my tongue since I was a child at home..."

"What did they say? What did you learn?"

"There is no bomb, Burt! It was all a bluff—they didn't dare to use explosives...it would have the same effect as the dumping, and cost them their own lives...we're not all martyrs, Burt..." She began to sob openly now.

"Dr. Nichols," she said at last. "He's dead, Burt...he couldn't make the cruiser...he couldn't hold out..."

"Jessie, listen! I'm going to report this to Colihan immediately. We'll radio again soon."

"Be careful, Burt! Please be careful!"

Burt went to the wardroom.

They stopped their conversation when they saw his eyes.

"Dr. Nichols is dead," he told them. "There isn't any bomb below the ship. We can dump the cans..."

"It's a lie!" Crofter shrieked, "It's a damned lie!"

He told them the story. They left the room quickly, to start the process of unloading the deadly cargo they carried.

Burt went to the porthole, and saw the nose of the cruiser outlined against the dark sky.

On the deck, he heard the first splash that signaled the end of life in Marracott Deep.

THE END

If you've enjoyed this book, you will not want to miss these terrific titles...

ARMCHAIR SCI-FI & HORROR DOUBLE NOVELS, $12.95 each

D-1 **THE GALAXY RAIDERS** by William P. McGivern
SPACE STATION #1 by Frank Belknap Long

D-2 **THE PROGRAMMED PEOPLE** by Jack Sharkey
SLAVES OF THE CRYSTAL BRAIN by Rog Phillips

D-3 **YOU'RE ALL ALONE** by Fritz Leiber
THE LIQUID MAN by Bernard C. Gilford

D-4 **CITADEL OF THE STAR LORDS** by Edmond Hamilton
VOYAGE TO ETERNITY by Milton Lesser

D-5 **IRON MEN OF VENUS** by Don Wilcox
THE MAN WITH ABSOLUTE MOTION by Noel Loomis

D-6 **WHO SOWS THE WIND...** by Rog Phillips
THE PUZZLE PLANET by Robert A. W. Lowndes

D-7 **PLANET OF DREAD** by Murray Leinster
TWICE UPON A TIME by Charles L. Fontenay

D-8 **THE TERROR OUT OF SPACE** by Dwight V. Swain
QUEST OF THE GOLDEN APE by Paul W. Fairman and Milton Lesser

D-9 **SECRET OF MARRACOTT DEEP** by Henry Slesar
PAWN OF THE BLACK FLEET by Mark Clifton.

D-10 **BEYOND THE RINGS OF SATURN** by Robert Moore Williams
A MAN OBSESSED by Alan E. Nourse

ARMCHAIR SCIENCE FICTION CLASSICS, $12.95 each

C-1 **THE GREEN MAN**
by Harold M. Sherman

C-2 **A TRACE OF MEMORY**
By Keith Laumer

C-3 **INTO PLUTONIAN DEPTHS**
by Stanton A. Coblentz

ARMCHAIR MASTERS OF SCIENCE FICTION SERIES, $16.95 each

M-1 **MASTERS OF SCIENCE FICTION, Vol. One**
Bryce Walton—"Dark of the Moon" and other tales

M-2 **MASTERS OF SCIENCE FICTION, Vol. Two**
Jerome Bixby—"One Way Street" and other tales

A MASSIVE ALIEN FLEET HOVERS IN THE SKIES ABOVE EARTH

An alien invasion of Earth? It was almost incomprehensible. For many long days, though, the grim, threatening spaceships of the invading alien armada hovered in the skies above every major city, washing the earth and the people below in a stinking miasma of impending, evil dread.

The world waited…

Then suddenly the pattern stopped and the people of Earth stood in fearful anticipation of the Aliens' next move.

Here is a classic sci-fi tale from the 1960s of an impending alien invasion— only with a different twist.

CAST OF CHARACTERS

RALPH KENNEDY
The military needed him because he was the number one man in extraterrestrial psychology. There was only one problem—he wasn't the man they thought he was!

HARVEY STRICKLAND
He was the Czar in world communications and public opinion. Naturally the Starmen would enter into a dialogue with him first…wouldn't they?

THE STARMEN
Friend or Foe? Were these strange visitors to Earth honorable heroes or directors of an elaborate hoax?

DR. FREDERICK KIBBIE
Director of the Department of Extraterrestrial Life Research. Not a big believer in ET, but definitely on board with gaining funds to study them.

SARA
Kennedy's loyal secretary, she raised eyebrows when she eagerly followed her boss to his new appointment in Washington.

SHIRLEY CHASE
She knew the in's and out's of the political scene in Washington—and Kennedy was be lost without her.

PAWN OF THE BLACK FLEET

By
MARK CLIFTON

ARMCHAIR FICTION
PO Box 4369, Medford, Oregon   97501-0168

PROLOGUE

DEEP within the spiralling galaxy, seen edge-on from Earth as the Milky Way, the thought channels summoned the regular members of the Interstellar Galaxy Council into communion.

"Our detection traps have been sprung."

"Another life form is stirring within the egg of its solar system."

"It has already spread from its mother planet cell to other cells within the egg."

"It may soon crack the shell, break through the insulating distance, spread out among the stars!'

"Encountering our own cultures."

"Let us not be premature. It may prove stillborn. Never discover how to leave its egg, and destroy itself by its own growth within."

"But again, it may break through at any time. It need only discover the principle of the interstellar drive. So many have."

"Or, as among some of us, transcend mechanics entirely and learn how to transport or transmute the material, or the illusion of the material, by wish alone."

"To appear among us instantaneously."

"Unprepared for community responsibility."

"We do not know if this new life form is virulent or benign."

"Probably just adolescent."

"Virulent, then."

"Some study in how to protect ourselves from it is indicated. Are we agreed?"

"Yes. Summon the Five."

I SUPPOSE it is the usual survey job?"

"Council seems to think so."

"Best follow regular procedure; go right into the egg; remain undetected until we know the problem. Then appear, or not appear to them, as needed."

"Assuming their adolescence. That means they'll be more concerned with asserting than with learning. We'll need to gain their confidence if we appear."

"Not always easy to gain the confidence of an adolescent. His standards are not necessarily logical."

"But always naïve. Rescue him from peril and you are his friend. Ridiculous, but it does work."

"The trick is to find out what he considers peril."

"Threat to his survival, usually."

PAWN of the BLACK FLEET

By MARK CLIFTON

Illustrated by FINLAY

For days the grim, threatening spaceships of the invading armada appeared simultaneously over every major city, washing the earth below in a stinking miasma of revolting, evil dread. Then suddenly, the pattern stopped and the world waited silently, fearfully, for the next move.

"But the semantics of the threat varies."

"His art forms usually reveal the semantics of his mores. If they've sprung the detection traps they undoubtedly have electronically distributed art forms."

"Reshape our outer forms into the approved symbols revealed by his art forms, faithfully follow the pattern."

"Yes, that usually works."

"Wait a while, I've been vectoring this new disturbance. I seem to recall from the archives of some culture somewhere that there were some recent visitations to that area."

"How could there be? It's strictly violation of Galaxy Council's rule to make unauthorized visits and we Five are always sent in first to make the initial survey."

"That brings it to mind. It was Vega. The fourth planet of Vega. The one who broke through the barrier before Council estimated they were ready. On their own they did some exploration of that section. The Vegans were still pretty primitive in some aspects."

"Still are."

"Well, they do admittedly still have a malicious streak in their character. Anyhow, they appeared before this lower life form as super-beings, and got quite a kick out of impressing them with magic tricks. Childish behavior, of course, and Council soon put a stop to it."

"But damage could have been done. If it is the same place we could find a really messed up semantic development."

"Might not be the same one. Hardly see how a life form could have progressed to the science of atomics if it were all messed up with belief in super being magic—the unlogic of unreality behavior."

"Hope it wasn't the same culture. Such a messy problem."

"We'll have to study their art form communication patterns carefully before we reveal ourselves. The meddling Vegans could have complicated the problem."

"Probably wasn't this culture at all. They've got nuclear fission and fusion. They've got interplanetary travel. We know they've got that, and they couldn't have if they hadn't at least some accurate estimations of reality."

"So they must be rational, after all."

The silken sough of sighing whirled infinity.

"Yes, of course. You're right. They're already rational!"

CHAPTER ONE

THE scene in my waiting room was usual that June morning when I came, a little late, into my office. It was just after graduation and the benches and chairs were filled with young cybernetics engineers, primed by their college instructors to tell us what was wrong with our Company and how it ought to be operated—for a fabulous salary, of course. In the meantime they were waiting for someone to help them solve the hopeless puzzle of our application form—revised and simplified version—or to tell them how to spell "Yes" and "No".

"There's an important letter on your desk, Mr. Kennedy," my pretty receptionist called out in a voice louder than necessary as I approached her desk. I may have looked a little startled. Normally, we do not parade the mechanics of operating our Personnel Department before the applicants. And, too, it was usually reserved for Sara, my secretary, to break the news of what would face me that day.

"It's from the Pentagon," the receptionist prattled on loudly, but her eyes were covertly on the applicants. I got the message then. Lucky applicants! to be hired by a Company who has an Executive who gets mail from the Pentagon!

"It's marked Personal, Private, Confidential, Urgent, and…"

"Why don't you get yourself a loud speaker, girl," I murmured out of one corner of my mouth as I started to pass her desk.

"Aw, give 'em a thrill, boss," she murmured back through tight lips. "Think of all those years of deadly monotony ahead of them if they do get hired."

"All right, all right!" I cooperated a little loudly, myself. "Now what does that Pentagon want?" I shrugged impatiently.

I really wasn't very impressed. It was probably a poster they wanted pinned on our bulletin board telling our young men to quit their jobs and join Space Navy to see the universe. Which would be stretching it a bit, because we were still planning that supreme effort which would get us out as far as Jupiter's moons.

I walked on through the open door into my secretary's office, which was a buffer zone between me and the crude, rough world outside. Sara was alert and grinning as she sat behind her own desk. She held up a letter knife, handle toward me.

"You may open it all by yourself," she said with her characteristic burlesque of secretarial concern. "With all those red cautions stamped on it, I didn't dare. It's laying right on top of your desk."

I grinned back at her, took the knife and went on into my own office. The letter lay on an otherwise clean and polished surface: I slit the envelope and pulled out a single folded sheet.

It wasn't a poster.

I slid my eyes past the quarter page of protocol, file and reference numbers, to the first paragraph. Halfway through the first sentence I sat down in my chair, rather heavily.

Dear Mr. Kennedy:

Pursuant to your application for the position of Staff Psychologist, specializing in the adaptation of Extraterrestrial Beings to Earth Ecology, your appointment is hereby confirmed.

You are ordered to report to Dr. Frederick Kibbie, Director of the Department of Extraterrestrial Life Research, Space Navy, Pentagon, promptly at 900 22-June-annum.

Inasmuch as this appointment automatically constitutes an Acting Commission in Space Navy (pending personal investigation of your sex practices by F. B. I.) failure to comply with this order will be prima facie evidence of willful disobedience of military orders by a commissioned officer in time of war emergency; an act of high treason; the exact penalties to be later fixed by formal Courts Martial.

Cordially yours, and my personal warmest congratulations.

STAR ADMIRAL HERBERT LYTLE
Space Navy
Personnel Director

I SAT and stared through the slits of venetian blind at the blank wall of our factory production unit across the street while I fumbled with a free hand for a sustaining cigarette.

It was a mistake, of course. Space Navy had got its files mixed up.

In the first place, I was plain Mister, not Doctor.

In the second place, I hadn't made any application to Space Navy for any kind of job.

Third, I wasn't a psychologist, let alone a specialist in the adaptation of Extraterrestrial Beings to Earth Ecology, whatever that might be. Frankly, I didn't see how there could be such a specialist since, so far, we hadn't discovered any Extraterrestrial Beings to adapt. And if we ever did, I wasn't sure who would have to do the adapting—they or us.

Fourth, there wasn't any war emergency, at least not that I'd heard of, and I'd surely have noticed the headlines while I was looking for the funnies.

Fifth, I didn't think it was any of the F. B. I.'s business what I did with my sex life, even if I were going to work for government, which I wasn't.

Sixth, I didn't want a commission in any kind of Navy, Space or Puddle.

Seventh—neither did I wish to be Court-Martialled for high treason by not showing up in precisely forty-eight hours.

In military style, that seemed to have ticked off the reasons why it must be a mistake. I need only communicate these points to Space Navy to straighten it out. I crushed out my cigarette and reached for the telephone.

Of course I didn't get to Star Admiral Herbert Lytle, who had welcomed me with such warm personal cordiality, but I did get as far as the clerk-yeoman in charge of the department of files handling names beginning in K.

There was a delay, Computer Research expense, while this fellow went to find my file. From three thousand miles away I could visualize his every movement while he searched the files where my dossier ought to be—but wasn't. From my own long experience in Personnel Offices, I could have told him to arrange a conference of the various department heads to have their staffs look under D for Doctor, Ra for Ralph, or in the Star Admiral's bottom desk drawer, his secretary's IN tray, OUT tray, wastebasket; or in possession of a contingent of Shore Patrolmen already on their way to arrest me.

But the clerk-yeoman fooled me. He came back on the wire and started talking, rapidly.

"Now you listen here, Doctor Kennedy," he began severely—although he made me feel at home to note his voice did contain those overtones of hysteria, which are a trademark among personnel clerks. "We absolutely cannot consider a stay of time in your case. Your personal inconvenience is of small consequence compared with the needs of the United States Government, Space Navy, and our responsibility to keep the Universe under control. This lack of discipline and proper attitude from you civilians..."

"There's-been-a-mistake!" I managed to shout him down.

THERE was complete silence, catatonic shock silence. It was broken by an impatient long distance operator.

"Are you still on the line?" she asked crisply.

"*I* am," I answered patiently. "I suspect the party at the other end may have fainted."

The clerk-yeoman came back on the wire at that point. Now his voice was slow, ominous. He quoted my social security number at me. I checked my wallet, found my card among my status symbols, and admitted to him it was my number. He quoted my middle name, without laughing. I confessed to it. He told me my mother's maiden name. I admitted he had me pegged down, but I made another try.

"You've got the right data," I said. "But the wrong man. Somewhere in these United States there must be a Doctor Kennedy who wants that job and you've got the files mixed up."

There was a gasp at the other end of the line.

"Then why would we have your file at all?" he asked.

"Don't ask me how you should run your office," I snapped back. "Computer Research, where I work, has had a lot of past dealings with the Pentagon. I've had personal brushes with quite a few high-ranking officers in various branches. Doubtless someone, sometime, has run up a dossier on me, and that's the one you've got. But I'm not a Doctor Kennedy. I'm a plain Mister Kennedy. It makes a difference."

"Certainly it makes a difference." His tone was growing waspish now. "Space Navy does not hand out commissions to any status level below that of Doctor. Star Admiral Lytle has given you a commission. Therefore you must be the correct Doctor Kennedy."

"Then Lytle has made the mistake," I said reasonably.

There was a double gasp this time. "I'm to tell *Star Admiral* Lytle *he* has made a mistake?" he asked. "Oh my God," he groaned. "This is what comes of making civilians into commissioned officers. A Star Admiral does not make mistakes. He cannot make mistakes. The Space Navy does not make mistakes. It cannot make mistakes. You are therefore Doctor Kennedy, *the* correct Doctor Kennedy, and all this is an evasion, a subterfuge you are using to avoid performing your patriotic duty to your country."

He paused for breath; and when his voice came again it was a full octave lower in tone.

"You will report at the designated time and place of your own free will," he said slowly. "Or you will report in irons. It makes no difference to me."

He hung up.

I hung up, too, slowly. I'd better go see Old Stone Face, Mr. Henry Greenbelt, the General Manager. He had also had a lot of past dealings with the Pentagon, and at levels higher than my contacts. Maybe he could help.

CHAPTER TWO

OLD Stone Face, at his half acre of desk and surrounded by the rich walnut panels glowing warm in the muted indirect light, was confident that one telephone call would straighten it all out for me. I didn't often ask his help in running my department, to say nothing of my personal affairs, and he seemed glad to demonstrate how much weight he could swing around the Pentagon.

But as the series of frustrating telephone calls wore into the morning, he progressed from high confidence, to exasperation, to self-disciplined patience, to bewilderment, to anger, to defeat.

He sat back finally in his overstuffed chair, beetled his heavy brows, and peered at me suspiciously across the desk.

"You *say* you didn't apply for the job. Let's *say* I believe you."

I straightened up from a weary slouch, and raised my hand in the scout oath position.

"Wouldn't have done you any good if you had," he rumbled from somewhere down in the granite facade. "After some of the things you've done to some of those officers, you'd have been turned down like a shot. They all agree with me that the sheer safety of our nation depends on keeping you away from the Pentagon."

"Well then?" I asked.

"So they're all hot to intercede until I mention it is Space Navy. Then they cool down a bit. And when I mention it's the Extraterrestrial Psychology Department they back off and want no part of trying to spring you. Sanfordwaithe says maybe they need you in that Department after all, that no sacrifice is too great for the rest of the Pentagon, if... He didn't say, if what. But something's going on, and they're all mighty skittish about it."

"So what'm I going to do?" I asked.

"Guess you'd better make the trip," he said slowly. "Somehow I think maybe Computer Research wouldn't have to close its doors if you were gone for a day or so. You go see this bird, this Kibbie fellow. You tell him, in person, you're not the man he thought you were. Soon as he sees you, he'll believe it. But it looks like it has to be in person. I can't get even a general or an admiral to so much as call him on the phone."

"So I suppose I'd better go," I admitted. "On expense account?"

He rared up at that.

"It's your personal neck," he roared. "Why should the Company have to pay for saving it?"

"Now, Henry." I looked at him and shook my head sadly.

"Oh, all right. I'll set it up. I was going to, anyway." There was a fleeting crack in the granite of his face.

"I wonder what's going on?" he mused thoughtfully, and put his fingertips together. "There's something they're not telling us. You find out what it is, Ralphie, my boy."

I sprang up out of my chair as if I'd been stung.

"Yeah," I said bitterly, glaring down at him. "And see if we can't get the job of making a computer to solve it, whatever it is.

You couldn't possibly pay my expenses just because it's me; just because of all the years I've worked my heart out for dear old Computer Research."

I whirled around angrily and started for the door. His voice, slow and measured, followed me, stopped me.

"We got a Board of Directors," he was saying. "We got Stockholders. If it took one lousy nickel out of their pockets to save you, they'd see you hang without batting an eye. You know that, well as I do. But now, say, suppose it was my best judgement to send you to Washington to drum up some more business..."

I turned around and stared at him, incredulous. Far down in the glacial ice blue of his eyes, I thought I detected the faintest possible gleam of affection.

He stood up and came around the desk. He held out his hand. It was a momentous occasion. In all the years, I couldn't remember having shaken hands with him before. Looking back, now, I wonder if he had some premonition, even then, that I wouldn't be back. I hadn't. Even with all my experience in dealing with the military, I was still thinking it was a little error I could clear up with a few words of explanation once I got to the right person.

By the time I reached Washington and the Pentagon building I had only thirty-seven hours to find the right department, which was shaving it pretty fine.

Even Space Navy, after another long hassle of my trying to tell them I wasn't Doctor Kennedy, and they stubbornly maintaining that I was; and the still longer procedures of signing me in and clearing me for low level security, weren't sure they ought to let me in on the secret of how to find Dr. Frederick Kibbie.

But they were damned sure they would Courts-Martial me if I didn't find him. Something was, indeed, going on.

SECURITY prevents me from Revealing The Word of how to find the Department of Extraterrestrial Life Research in the Pentagon. Not that the top hierarchy of Russia doesn't know where it is down to the square inch, but John Q. Public, who pays the bills, mustn't be told.

And there are reasons.

Take away the trappings of Security Regulations, and our special qualifications to meet them, and what have we got left to mark us as superior to the common herd? It's a status symbol, pure and simple, and the gradations from Confidential on up to Q. S. have nothing whatever to do with enemy spies—they merely mark the status relationship of the elect within the select. And, after this passage of events I am about to relate, since I am now one of the, THE, Q. S., and have the awesome weight of knowing things that even—well, I mustn't reveal who isn't allowed to know what I know—I guess that makes me pretty hot. Sometimes even Sara (yes, I had to send for her) begins to show signs of going Government in her attitude toward me.

But once inside the department door, it was pretty much the same as any other suite of offices. There was first an anteroom where a narrow eyed and suspicious young man examined the sheaf of credentials Space Navy Personnel had prepared for me while running me through their dehydrated equivalent of six weeks in boot camp. Reluctantly, he passed me on to the next anteroom where a secretary's secretary confirmed that I had an appointment. In the next room the Secretary, himself, pretended he'd never heard of me, and we had it all to go through again. Of course I insisted to each one of them that a mistake had been made, that I was the wrong man, that I should be turned away and not allowed to see Dr. Kibbie, and that may have hurried the process of letting me through.

Against my will, I liked Dr. Kibbie as soon as I stepped inside his office. He was rushed, but he was cordial. It was evident he had a thousand things on his mind, but he was willing to give me that thousandth part of his mind which was my rightful share.

He was about twenty years older than I, around fifty-eight to sixty, I'd say. I'm tall and thin, he was short and round. I'm dark haired and can still wear it in the young blade fashion of the day; he was shiny bald with a grey fringe around the sides and back. I'm inclined to be a little dour at times, so they tell me; he was as phoney happy and bouncy as a marriage counselor—and, at once, I suspected he was about as useful.

He had that open enthusiasm, that frank revealment of the superior con man as he told me all about his department and its four hundred employees.

Four hundred employees to do research on life forms which hadn't yet been discovered. I, personally, wouldn't have known what to do with them all, but this was government. They were all working like little beavers on fancy charts and graphs, statistics and analyses—covering something which doesn't exist—which is about par for government which models its approach to reality from the academic.

Mainly because I couldn't find a pause to interrupt, I let him finish the quick once over of his department, since it was apparent he liked to talk about all the wonderful things they were thinking of doing. Then I dropped my bomb.

I wasn't the right man for the job—whatever it might be!

Apparently that thousandth part of his mind he was giving me wasn't enough for him to grasp that I meant I was the wrong Kennedy.

"Now, now, now, Doctor!" he chattered absently, hurriedly. "We haven't time for the usual polite self-deprecations. All very commendable of course. Shows you had the proper training. Gives me confidence in you. Understand your reluctance to succeed where the rest of us have failed. Natural teamwork spirit. Commendable, most commendable. Ah yes, better to fail and keep the approval of your fellow scientists than to succeed and make enemies of them.

"Proper attitude. Most acceptable. Proud to have you on my team, Dr. Kennedy. Knew you were just the man. Knew that right away."

I leaned my elbow on his desk and braced my head with my hand. Too late, I realized what my procedure should have been. I should have told him I was eager for the job, just had to have it. That would have made him judiciously consider and reject me. I should have done it with Space Navy. Then they'd have been sure to find some reason why I couldn't make the grade.

"...proper humility, modesty," Kibbie was still rambling along. He whirled around and shook an admonitory finger at me, which made me lift my head again. "But that's all out now. For the duration. Can't afford to fail this time. Not even if the other scientists get annoyed with you for admitting that you know whatever it is you know. In a war emergency, individuals have to rise to self-sacrifice. Martyrdom!"

He paused to beam upon me proudly.

"What war emergency?" I was finally able to get down to the question.

"Why—ah—" he looked startled, and then came to a quick recapitulation of my state of ignorance. For a moment I thought the added burden might be too much for him, but he shouldered it manfully. He got up and took short, rapid steps over to the window where he gazed at the impressive row of shining white government buildings stretching to the horizon. There was a silence while he collected his thoughts. Apparently he decided I could take the full brunt of it, all at once.

"We're going out to Jupiter's moons!" He made the announcement portentous.

"Of course," I said, indifferently. "So?"

His face took on a hurt expression.

"You already know that?" he asked, disappointed.

"It's been in all the papers for days, weeks."

"Those Congressmen!" he exclaimed bitterly. "Always sucking up to news reporters, hoping they'll get their names in the papers or even mentioned on TV."

"But anybody could have figured it out," I consoled him. "We've already got contingents on Mars and Venus. We're not equipped to start mining the Asteroid belt just yet. The state of the art won't permit landing on Jupiter, itself. Naturally, its moons would be next."

"I suppose you're right," he agreed ruefully. "Not really much of a secret."

"But what has that got to do with a war emergency?" I asked curiously.

"Don't you see?" he admonished me, and shook his finger at me again. "We don't know much about those moons. What if there is some kind of life form there? What if it is technically advanced? What if it is hostile? What if we weren't prepared? So—a war emergency!"

"Oh come now!" I made no secret of my disgust. "That's going pretty extreme, even if you had a military mind—which you haven't."

HE looked at me piercingly, and then his eyes began to twinkle.

"Shrewd!" he congratulated me. "Very shrewd. Oh I knew you were the right man for me. Doesn't take you in for a minute. Took in that Congressional Committee without a murmur of doubt. Secret session of course. Very, very hush-hush. I asked for four billion. They gave me only two billion, so, later when it can be told, they can show the voters how economy minded they were. Paid me two billion dollars, well, for running my department, of course, for the status satisfaction of being in on something nobody else knows. In open session they wouldn't have given me a dime."

"So the war emergency is just a con," I said.

He paced the floor for a moment more. His face was serious, drawn in worry.

"No," he said, at last. "It's real." He came across the room to stand at my elbow. "So now I'll tell you the real reason. The one known to the top men here in the Pentagon. The one we couldn't tell Congress because they're such blabbermouths, and so we had to con them. Mustn't leak this to the reporters, son," he began in a warning. "Public mustn't know, mustn't find out."

"Why?" I asked.

He drew a quick breath.

"Oh my! Oh my! You really are from the Outside! Have to do something about that Outside attitude, right away. You're in government now. First rule of government of the people, by the people, for the people: Never tell the people!"

He came over, stood in front of me, and peered at me with narrowed eyes. Apparently he was waiting for a loyalty oath. I raised my fingers in scout's honor. It seemed to satisfy him.

"The Black Fleet has struck four times!" he whispered hoarsely.

"The WHAT?" I shouted.

"Sh-h-h!" he put his fingers to his lips hurriedly, and looked around the room.

"The what?" I asked, more normally.

"The Black Fleet."

"What the hell is the Black Fleet?"

He snapped his fingers in delight.

"Good! Oh, good! Then that news hasn't leaked yet. Sometimes those generals and admirals are as anxious to get their names in the paper as a Congressman." He was as delighted as a child successfully playing button-button.

"Tell you all about it," he said. He came back and settled down at his desk.

"Best if we start at the beginning," he said. "We'll review the charts and analyses of all my departments on it. You're going to need to know every detail. Because, as the expert in Extraterrestrial Psychology, that's your job.

"To interpret what it all means.

"To find out who they are.

"What they are.

"What they're up to."

I waited, for he had spaced each item with a long impressive pause, and wasn't finished.

"And how we can drive them off before the people find out that Earth has been invaded!"

CHAPTER THREE

THE announcement proved more impressive than the evidence.

Dr. Kibbie's staff tried. He combined introduction of his various department heads with a full dress presentation of their material; but since neither then nor later did I have more than the most casual relations with the men, their names remained only names.

This half dozen or so assorted names brought in their charts and graphs, and charts and graphs explaining their charts and graphs. They produced maps and statistics and analyses, and analyses of maps and statistics and analyses. As the office walls, tables, desks, and even the floor became littered with these impressive evidences of loving labor, I began to get the feeling I was in a room of mirrors, where images of images were being repeated to infinity.

One such chart I remember as being a prototype of most. It was the pride and joy of Dr. Er-Ah. Meticulously, beautifully drafted, it covered an entire worktable. He went to some pains to assure me that this was only the working copy, that the master remained locked in their vault except at times it was mandatory to make further entries upon it, after such entries had been charted and approved on the working copy.

The purple vertical lines represented the hours. The red vertical lines represented the minutes. If I cared to verify the chart's accuracy, I would find there were always fifty-nine red lines in between the bolder purple lines. The still bolder black horizontal line represented the actual passage of time through the minutes and hours. The dotted pencil line, stretching out beyond the black horizontal, represented the *prediction* of time passage through the minutes and hours of the future.

WITH almost uncanny accuracy, Dr. Er-Ah could predict that when so many minutes in the future had passed, a given number of hours would also have passed! It was now eleven o'clock. When sixty more minutes had passed, his chart revealed that there was strong probability that it would be twelve o'clock!

Now I began to get the idea how four hundred people could be kept busy, but I was not to woolgather about it, for he was not finished.

His clerks would fill in the bold black line, as each minute passed, to check the accuracy of his prediction. When this had been properly checked and verified and authorized, the master copy could be taken out of the vault and brought up to date with the working copy. Of course I appreciated that while he had the working copy tied up in here for review, his department was being greatly handicapped, and would probably have to work overtime to catch up the delay in their work.

HE reached his moment of triumph when I inquired what this had to do with extraterrestrial psychology.

"When, and if, another life form is discovered," Dr. Er-Ah instructed gravely, "the instant will be marked on this chart, and finally on the master chart in the vault, as a permanent record for all posterity." As one of the most momentous events in all mankind's history, I could appreciate the necessity for absolute accuracy when I realized that historians of the future for thousands of years, tens and hundreds of thousands of years, must refer back to this historic chart for an absolute fix.

The dedicated vision, which makes some few scientists great, shone from his visage.

Nor was Dr. Kibbie far behind in exaltation. Here, surrounded by the months of work which had gone into this display, each piece of which made valiant effort to equal the time chart in workmanship and usefulness, the man came into his own. Now I began to realize why a Congressional Committee had paid out two billion dollars. They are not the only ones to assume that charts and graphs must mean something.

Even more, I appreciated Dr. Kibbie's motive in keeping four hundred people busy accomplishing absolutely nothing. The status of a government official depends entirely upon his title and the number of people he supervises. It has nothing whatever to do with what he accomplishes, or whether anything at all is ever accomplished—the academic transferred to the government.

And Dr. Kibbie was determined to become a most important man.

I found myself wanting to believe in all this impressive work—a work of which I now, somehow, had become a part. Kibbie had that quality about him. There was no doubt now that he was a first class con man, active where the pickings are richest. He had already conned Congress out of two billion for nothing, and even granting the traditional Congressional habit of shoveling out tax millions for wild-haired schemes while withholding pennies from sound and sorely needed projects, it was still quite a con feat. I suspected it was only a beginning.

I wanted to believe, to become a True Believer like the rest of his department. But obviously, I must still be thinking as an Outsider; for, boiled down to essentials, all the charts and graphs and analyses added up to little more than some of the vaguer flying saucer reports.

IN the central Ural Mountains of Russia, some goat herders had seen a fleet of black flying saucers hovering overhead. A red ray had licked down and melted away one of the peaks to make it run like a river. That was the sum and substance.

Some of their kids had brought the hallucination of their ignorant parents to the district school where it could be exposed by the analysis of dialectic materialism. Ever alert to the evil machinations of the Wall Street Overlords, even while the teachers felt it best to soothe and explain away the superstition for their students, they, nonetheless, forwarded the information through the proper channels to the Propaganda Ministry. Possibly there was hope of reminding the peace-loving people of Russia of their danger by this latest invasion of the Capitalist Royalists and their Boot Licking Lackeys.

The Propaganda Ministry sent out some of its best propagandists to the Urals, and among them, of course, was one of our own C. I. A. operatives.

But when they got there, the parents had been convinced by their more enlightened children that either they hadn't seen what they knew they had seen, or had better keep their mouths shut about it. The reports and evidence were too evasive, tenuous and vague, even for Kremlin purposes, and nothing more would have been heard of it—except that the C. I. A. operative felt it necessary to include a summary in his report to substantiate his expense account. He did see fit to add a footnote, a rather extensive footnote, to provide our own propagandists with whatever color background they might find useful.

As for example, although this was now fourth generation under Communism's dialectic materialism, the backward peasants—er, enlightened Comrade-Workers—had been unable to separate natural from supernatural. With the excellent police training he had received here in the United States, he had succeeded in inciting them into committing the crime they had not intended to commit. Because he succeeded in convincing them he was one of them at heart, they confessed to him, in secret, how they had felt toward the phenomenon. They had dwelt heavily upon the semantics of Evil, as a palpable force, which emanated from the Black Fleet. Fear and hatred of the Fleet had swept over them, appalled and frozen them in their tracks, even before the emission of the red ray.

Perhaps it was this hint of the supernatural seeping through which made the Russian propagandists feel more was to be lost than gained through making something of it all and which caused them to hush up the whole thing. But maybe ours could find it useful to show that you can't educate primeval superstition out of man through appeals to logic and reason—or however sentimentally and culturally acceptable our own propagandists might want to phrase it.

Whether there actually had been a Black Fleet and a red ray, to say nothing of its having been a materialization of the forces of Evil, was not for the C. I. A. man to say. He, he said, reported only facts. The sense of Evil was one of those facts. As for the rest, he had truly seen a level mountain table of hardened lava with octopus tentacles running down adjacent ravines.

THERE seemed to be a discrepancy in time. Where a chance of influencing world opinion is concerned, the Russian government can move fast. They are indifferent only to the welfare of their own citizens, and it is only there that months and years of bureaucratic red-tape intervene between the need for a pair of shoes and getting them. The Propaganda Ministry had moved fast. The peasants claimed a sharply pointed mountain peak had stood there only one week before. But the lava was quite cold and hard, and couldn't have lowered its temperature to that of the surrounding untouched rock in so short a time. Since no government office maintained an accurate time chart in that area; or at least no Dr. Kibbie trained scientist of the calibre of Dr. Er-Ah maintained one, the time it had happened, if it had happened at all was inconclusive.

I personally, thought "inconclusive" was just the word to describe the whole thing.

This was the most detailed and authentic of the reports. As to actual details, it seemed to me the C. I. A. man must be bucking for a transfer to writing propaganda instead of collecting facts. I was prepared for the remaining reports to be even more vague and inconclusive. They were.

There was one from the interior of the Sahara Desert, to wind up as gossip in an Oasis Bazaar; but since the tribesmen had departed with their caravan and no one knew who they were by the time our C. I. A. man got onto it (his Arabic was too weak and the palm wine too strong) there was no way of checking the facts.

Another came from deep in the Andes, reported by some mountain Indians; but since this was South America which knew better than to cause any trouble for the United States we had no C. I. A. operative on the spot. The report had filtered down to the coast, and was picked up there by some government operatives masquerading as Maritime Union sailors. In due course it, too, had filtered into the Department of Extraterrestrial Psychology because it seemed to be something about possible visitors from outer space. Even this department didn't consider it iron clad evidence.

The fourth report came from some all but deserted South Sea Island; brought in to Tahiti by some itinerate Polynesian fishermen who had somehow escaped from Tourist Entertainment Service, and were therefore low characters not to be trusted.

I did have to credit the significance of an almost identical rumor coming from widely separated sources, all at about the same time, and two of them not reported by C. I. A. operatives, and therefore not necessarily planned to please the boss, the press, or to increase world tensions and protect their jobs.

A Fleet of black, disc shaped Things hovering overhead. A red ray licks down and destroys something, a mountain peak, a sweep of sand dunes, a mountain peak again, a deserted island. And the horror, the stunning and freezing horror of Evil, malignant Evil. That, most of all.

Even granting that the reports had, by the time I saw them, already been manipulated by the hands of analysts and statisticians, the similarities caught me.

I was far from sure, however, that there was sufficient meat for me to carry out my assignment—how to say who they were, what they were, what they were up to.

And how we could drive them away without anybody learning about it.

By mid-afternoon the various Dr. Er-Ah's carted away their treasured evidence and I was left once more, with Dr. Kibbie for whose ears alone my valuable judgement was reserved.

He leaned forward over his desk and looked at me alertly, brightly, hopefully, expectantly. I didn't have the heart to disappoint him.

"Interesting," I breathed. "Ve-e-ery interesting! But without further corroborative studies, sampling statistics, and analyses of your analyses..." I trailed off vaguely in the approved scientific manner.

He beamed in satisfaction.

"I'll need an office," I said.

"Already set aside for you," he answered. "I'll show it to you before you leave for the hotel where we've reserved a suite for you. That way you can come right to work in the morning without the delay of coming to me, first. I'm really quite busy, and time, time is precious."

"I'll need a staff."

"Already requisitioned from the government employee pool," he said promptly, and anticipated my approval of his efficiency in providing for all my needs. I nodded appreciatively. "Your staff is limited to three people as a start," he added apologetically. "That's standard procedure."

"Enough to start with," I conceded; and then decided that so long as I seemed to have no choice about becoming a government official. I might as well be an important one—by their standards. And the more important I became, the more important he would become, since he was my boss. "But only as a start," I continued. "The work I foresee may well require two or three hundred. Maybe more."

"That's the ticket!" he exclaimed. "Think big! Oh I can see we have the right man. I'll confess I've been a little disappointed in some of my Division Heads. Good scientists all. The Best. But perhaps, administratively, their vision has been limited."

I decided to see just where that limit might be.

"Before I'm through," I warned. "My needs may run into thousands of people."

I thought of Old Stone Face. Computer Research already seemed far away, a tiny speck down there somewhere from these Olympian Heights. Of course I'd have to call him, let him know I'd turned out to be the right man after all. I might even throw him a little business to clear him with his Board of Directors and Stockholders—grubby little businessmen, but the source of tax monies.

"And equipment," I continued. "I may need some specially designed computers—in fact I may even need a Brain."

He looked thoughtful, cautious.

"There's only two billion available at present," he warned me. "And Congress is not in session just now."

"I know a company which might be able to stay somewhere within that figure," I said.

"Don't tell me the name," he said hurriedly. "Must remember you're an important governmental official now (or will be important when you've hired all those people and spent all that money). You have a responsibility to the taxpayers not to use anything you have learned outside of government service. Where to get the proper computer would be that kind of misuse of special knowledge."

He shoved a memo pad toward me.

"Here," he said. "Don't trust your memory. You'll have too many things on your mind to remember such a detail. Jot the name down on a pad. Just for your own use if the need ever arises: Press hard, so my lab boys won't have too much trouble in bringing up the impressions from the pages below the one you tear off."

He beamed at me, as if to approve that I was already learning, fast, how to be a government man.

CHAPTER FOUR

NATURALLY I had no choice in selecting my staff personnel. It was well I hadn't, for I was to learn that knowing the ropes of red tape and protocol was far more important than any possible skill or efficiency learned on the Outside.

When I arrived the following morning at the departmental suite, which had been set aside for me, temporary quarters until we outgrew the space, I found the door had already been lettered:

BUREAU OF EXTRATERRESTRIAL LIFE RESEARCH
DIVISION OF EXTRATERRESTRIAL PSYCHOLOGY
DEPARTMENT OF EXTRATERRESTRIAL VOCATIONAL
RESEARCH
DIRECTOR
Dr. Ralph Kennedy

Apparently my real mission was to be concealed. Ostensibly my job was to train extraterrestrials vocationally and put them to work in self-respecting employment—if we ever did discover any.

My real mission, of course, was to drive them away before anybody found out they'd been here; but I correctly suspected my staff would not know why they were really hired and what they were really supposed to help me do.

When I opened the door, I found that staff already busy at work. It consisted of a middle-aged woman and two reasonably young men.

Their desks were already piled high with file folders, yard long printed forms with such ample blank spaces that it would take many hours to fill them out, and thick sheaves of bound reports. Some extra desks in the big, barn-like workroom had imposing charts, graphs and star maps in varicolored inks spread over them. It was a beehive of activity and gave the quick illusion of many, many more staff members who just happened to be away from their desks on important missions or in vital conferences at the time.

I suddenly realized that not only was the status of an official determined by how many people he commanded; but this, in turn, reflected upon the status of those working for him, as well. My staff of only three must have been feeling their unimportance keenly.

No one looked up when I entered the door. They were much too busy. Since I hadn't yet begun to plan the kind of work to keep them busy, even with the excellent examples I'd seen the day before, I marveled at their skill in looking so frantically overworked so soon. But then, I was still thinking as an industry man, and, instead, I must immediately requisition some more help to lift the burden from their overworked backs.

THERE was a long, high counter between me and the area where they sat. Standard equipment where common citizens could stand and wait to be noticed. At one end was a gate for entrance into the sanctuary—with an angry notice on it telling me what Federal Law I would break and how many years penal servitude I'd risk if I entered without permission.

I tried the gate and found it locked.

I went and stood patiently at the counter.

When I didn't go away, the woman finally lifted her head and looked at me with exasperation; then pointedly returned her eyes to her work.

Central Personnel had filled my requirements without prejudice. They had given me thoroughly typical Civil Service Clerks.

"Who takes care of the cash customers?" I asked conversationally, after I'd stood another two minutes.

The woman lifted her head and stared at me with a level, intimidating gaze. Her face was thin and narrow; with sharp, neurotic lines running from the sides of her nose up to the corners of her piercing eyes. She could well have posed for a painting: Government Career Woman after Thirty Years.

"You will not be able to see Dr. Kennedy today," she said firmly. "He is much too busy."

"I'm Kennedy," I said mildly. "I'd just like to come through the gate so I can go to my office."

THE two male heads lifted then and looked me over. The woman got up and stalked over to release the catch.

"*Doctor* Kennedy," she acknowledged and at the same time reproved me for not using my title. "You have a private entrance to your office farther down the hall. The one marked 'No admittance'."

"But the penalty printed below the no admittance is so severe," I said, "I didn't, dare use the door. I noticed it yesterday, when I looked over the joint."

"Surveyed the premises," the hornrimmed young man murmured with disgusted asperity. I looked at him as I walked through the open gate.

"Who are you?" I asked him.

It seemed a natural question at the time, but the woman's face flamed red, and she glared at me. Hornrims looked at her with a certain glint of malicious mischief. Apparently I had tried to reverse their status by asking his name first. The woman quickly repaired the ordained order of the cosmos.

"I'm Shirley Chase," she said quickly before he could answer. "Miss Shirley Chase. I'm Executive Clerical Administrator of the Department of Extraterrestrial Vocational Research, Division of Extraterrestrial Psychology, Bureau of Extraterrestrial Life Research!" Then she turned toward Hornrims.

"This is Doctor Gerald Gaffey, A.B., B.S., M.A., M.S., PhD., Abstract Vocational Research Director of the Department of Extraterrestrial, etc., etc., etc. In research matters he may answer directly to you if and when required. In Departmental routine matters, he is under my jurisdiction."

Dr. Gerald Gaffey nodded coolly at a point somewhere above my head. I tried the friendly approach.

"H-m-m," I said. "Research into vocational guidance for extraterrestrials, huh? You must have held some powerful jobs in industry to qualify for that!"

"I am a Harvard man," he answered frigidly.

I realized I simply must over come my provincial West Coast attitude of wanting to see what a man had done in life before I measured his worth.

"Well," I said judiciously. "That's even better, isn't it."

Apparently the introductions were over. Miss Chase indicated the corridor leading from the workroom to my office, as if to tell me I might enter that way—this time.

"I haven't met the remainder of my staff," I said, and looked at the young man over in the corner.

"Oh?" Miss Chase looked at me questioningly, and smiled thinly. She had just come to the realization that I had absolutely no sense of protocol or etiquette whatever, and wasn't deliberately offensive. "That's only an N-462."

N-462 stared at me with startled eyes, and didn't nod.

"And what do you do here?" I asked.

His surprise seemed blended with horror and he looked uncertainly toward Miss Chase, as if seeking a protector.

"He is an N-462," she repeated.

I gathered he was too far down the ladder of protocol to speak to me directly, and that if I had been an experienced government career man I'd have known what an N-462 does. I let it pass.

I WALKED on down the hallway to my office, went in, and sat down behind my desk. The top of it was clear. There were no mountains of work piled upon it to make me look frantically indispensable to the continuance of the nation.

It told me, plainly, I was expected to build up my own fortress.

I had met my staff. I thought lonesomely, longingly of my staff back at Computer Research; a staff really busy doing necessary things, and at the same time dedicated to keeping my fortress intact for me. Apparently I did not yet have a private secretary. Apparently an official was permitted to choose his own.

Yes, of course, that would be it. And particularly for a bachelor. To make it easier for the F. B. I. to run its customary check on his sex practices. I would send for Sara.

I wondered which of my present staff was an undercover agent. Probably Miss Shirley Chase. Her breeding lines were unmistakably Mid-West out of New England, the classic picture of self appointed conscience for all mankind. I would have to watch my step around Shirley.

And thereby measured the real depth of my ignorance.

For eventually it turned out to be N-462; who wasn't really an N-462 at all. The gaffes that I had already pulled had sown the seeds of doubt in his mind about me. With that slow, patient, inexorable thoroughness of the truly great undercover man, he was to prove me only a Mister Ralph Kennedy, not the Doctor Kennedy at all.

An impostor!

CHAPTER FIVE

OF COURSE I was not naive enough to think that all the men around Washington played the national con-game of using the tax-payers as their own private herd of domestic animals with the same insouciant delight as Dr. Kibbie. His was the true gambler's attitude; that it is more fun to play for high stakes than for low, and not without status value among those who know the game; that sometimes you win, sometimes you lose; but basically you play just because there isn't anything else to do.

Nor were all others of the Dr. Gerald Gaffey stripe; academic theoreticians who had read a few books written vaguely about political science, listened to a few hours of even more vague professorial comments about it; and thought this was what governing a nation was all about.

Nor were the remaining all of that arrested mental development at the level of the twelve year old boy which manifests itself as the military mind. Most of my scraps with representatives of the Pentagon in the past were really seated in my disgust, tinged perhaps with a touch of horror, that grown men not only could allow their mental and spiritual development to be arrested at that juvenile age of running in gangs, hero worshipping, losing one's identity in marching conformity, hiding immature fears and weaknesses behind the bravado of brass and braid; but actually advocated this pitiful deformity as a way of life for others; and, indeed, brought all the weight and power of their massive gang disapproval to bear upon any who wished to outgrow such juvenile levels of value.

I knew there were still others. Not many, of these, for there was not room for many; and the sheer ferocity at this level kept their numbers from multiplying. To these Power was an end in itself, a compulsion, an addiction. Perhaps their need and fright was greatest of all, for only by acquisition of Power could they still their doubts that they were any different from the common domesticated herds of people. Only by applying and directing the aims of Power could they insure their own security. It had always been. It did not matter what the surface system of government was called in the fad notions of the time. There are those who milk, and those born to be milked.

Perhaps, in the still hours of the night, such men needed defense against an even greater enemy—their own intelligence. For that terrifying question hovered eternally just beyond recognition by their conscious minds, constantly threatened to verbalize itself in an unguarded moment: "What is the purpose of it all? What if there be no more purpose to human existence than to grass, or stone, or louse? How, then, could my ego ascend over others?"

I HAD not met such men. I did not expect to meet them. One doesn't. I might meet their boys, sometime—Congressmen, Senators, various administrators. Yes, I would surely meet their boys if I became any kind of threat to their husbandry.

There didn't seem to be much danger of that. Even in this unbelievable fantasy of official Washington, where everybody was PooBah, I couldn't seem to get into the spirit of things. I was nobody—and I knew it.

And yet...

I had seen how such men and their boys behaved when their counterparts over in Russia had tried to rustle some of their cattle from the pastures, or even scheme to highjack the lot of them—those fat, meaty cattle. I had seen what happened to those who got in the middle of this little private war over who shall milk them.

Now if there were...aw, ridiculous, of course...but, say, if there actually were beings who came from the stars; and if there were intentions of taking over the whole pasture and all the cattle in it.

Well!

I am Dr. Ralph Kennedy, Director of the Department of Extraterrestrial Vocational Research, Division of Extraterrestrial Psychology, Bureau of Extraterrestrial Life Research—with the secret mission of keeping them from doing it.

Right there in the middle.

CHAPTER SIX

THESE two little pieces of the jigsaw puzzle came to my attention much later; too late to be of any use. Although, in all honesty, even had I known these happenings in the Sheridan House, they would have carried no meaning to me. Only through hindsight would I have seen any connection between the reactions of a bellhop and The Black Fleet with the Red Ray. Later, the boys told me of their decision made in room 842, but had I actually been listening I doubt my reaction would have been much different from that of the bellhop.

Chronologically, however, the puzzle pieces fit in here.

Sheridan House, New York, was a moderately fashionable hotel on 64th Street, just off Central Park. The Night Manager, a shade more fashionable than even the hotel, was pleased with the evening. All was serene, and he was at his best in Serenity.

It was unfortunate that the bellhop had to mar the serenity. It was unfortunate that a hotel had to have bellhops.

In the late, late evening this bellhop shuffled across the lobby from the elevator and showed a pronounced list in his walk. There was a stringent rule that bellhops not drink on the job. The Night Manager pursed his lips ominously, and waited behind his hotel desk.

The bellhop leaned forward in his walk and made groping movements with his hands. There were large drops of sweat on his forehead, and his eyes protruded like those of a deep-sea fish suddenly hauled to the surface. When he reached the desk, he leaned his stomach against it and released his breath in a long, slow, fizzing sound.

"Jeez..." he breathed heavily.

The Night Manager stiffened further at this breach of manners, but he withheld reproof in the shocked realization that there was no alcohol in the generous waft of breath which came across the desk.

"Well, what is it?" he demanded. But his curiosity somewhat softened the intended tone of discipline.

The bellhop gulped and swallowed another mouthful of air.

"I—I better go home now."

The Night Manager's right eyebrow arched in skepticism. This was more familiar ground. Bellhops were always finding some reason why they couldn't finish out their shifts on slow, tipless nights.

"Must be my eyes, or my stomach," the bellhop whispered, awestricken. "I don't feel so good. Could I—uh—sit down somewhere?"

The Night Manager nodded toward his own office. He followed the bellhop and watched him collapse into a chair.

"What's the story this time?" he asked, and knew that curiosity had become ascendant to disbelief.

THE story came out in breathless spurts. A bar service call from 842. One Manhattan, one Old Fashioned. He had knocked on the door, quietly because it was getting late. He must have heard the command to enter. Must have heard it, although he couldn't remember hearing it. Anyway he entered. He didn't enter no rooms unless he was asked. Musta been asked.

"All right. All right!" the Night Manager prompted.

"One guy was sitting on the edge of the bed. Musta been a special bed, like some guests have to have, because it didn't sag none. I put the tray of drinks down on the table without looking around for anybody else. I'm just waitin' for my tip, see, and this guy's actin' like he don't know why I'm hangin' around for. You know the old cheapie routine, and then— It couldn't be my stomach, could it?" the bellhop broke off to plead.

"Never mind! We can do without your stomach."

"The bathroom door opens. I'm expectin' to see a dame. But this thing comes out."

"What thing?"

"This purple thing. Sort of a purple light in the shape of a whirlwind, or maybe water going down the drain."

"Then you have been drinking after all," the Night Manager exclaimed in disgust.

"Honest, Mr. Thistlewaithe. That's what it looked like. A purple whirlwind. It came floating across the room toward me and turned into about four other guys. Just like that! So help me! Next thing I know, it's only one other guy. But it's like a picture that's been exposed four times without moving only a little. One guy, only I could count him four times if you know what I mean."

"I don't. And I don't think you do."

"That's when I got outa there. He can have his lousy tip. Me, I'm sick at my stomach. I'm seein' things. Maybe it's my stomach, I think. Maybe it's…"

Mr. Thistlewaithe breathed a sigh of relief. Nothing to spoil his record of competency on his nightly report to top management. This was elementary; purely elementary to any student of psychology, and every hotel employee is at least that.

He faced the bellhop with a glow of anticipation. Now he could demonstrate why the bellhop was only a bellhop, while he was a Night Manager.

Reaching far back into the unfortunate lad's Freudian infancy, Mr. Thistlewaithe took off with a running start, sprinted through a sophomore psychology class at Columbia, soared through a pocketbook course in hallucination, spread his own theories concerning double brain lobe nonsynchronization and/or nerve synapses breaking circuit and instantaneously reclosing to create illusion of superimposure of memory upon memory; came down to earth again with a few digs about the effects of alcohol upon kidneys creating swimming sensations before the eyes; and broke the running record with dissertation on the shooting lights effects of cirrhosis of the liver.

A terrible thought struck him just as he breasted the finish line, and his voice trailed off. For although Mr. Thistlewaithe might be an accomplished avocationist in psychology, he was primarily a Night Manager. And it is his business to know the hotel floor plan, floor by floor; to know which rooms are occupied and which are not. And he was pretty sure that room 842 was empty. He rushed out of his office to the key rack. There were the two keys. He sped over to the empties list. The room was empty. He riffed through the day's registration cards. None showed a check-in to

842.

He turned and stared suspiciously at the bellhop.

The bellhop was not grinning.

IN 842 The Five, unregistered guests, were communing. They had correctly sommed this structure as shelter for travelers, and this room as unoccupied by any such travelers; but it had not occurred to them that one must register and pay. They could not yet grasp the idea that anywhere in the universe a life form could actually expect repayment for extending hospitality to a stranger. Indeed, the entire concept of commerce was still beyond their grasp. They knew of cannibalism, of course, but to find intelligent life feeding upon each other...

"What is this stuff you've chosen from the list of refreshments our host offers?"

"Basically alcohol. Its purpose is to deaden the senses."

"Why should any intelligent life wish to deaden its perceptions?"

"Oh, I don't know about that. If I were human, I think I might want my perceptions deadened permanently."

"You may have a point there. But then, have we found the intelligent species yet? In none of the random samples we've sommed..."

"No concept of atomic science. Yet, vague knowledge that other planets of this little solar system have been reached. But really not much interest in it, and no knowledge at all of how it was done. Well, a vague recognition of space ships, but no appreciation whatever of how they work, or how to build one."

"Yet space ships are built."

"So there must be an intelligent species, somewhere."

"Perhaps merely masquerading as a human being?"

"Why would they want to do that?"

"That's only one of the things we don't comprehend, yet."

"Our four Black Fleet strikes have come to nothing."

"I som only the vaguest telepathy communication in this species. Random, disorganized and undirected flashes."

"But they do have electronic communication. Highly

organized. Why weren't the visits of the Black Fleet electronically communicated?"

"We're in for quite a problem. We've always thought intelligence was characterized by the communication of knowledge. Here we find the emphasis is upon concealment of knowledge."

"The strikes of the Black Fleet were known. They were witnessed. We saw to that. I sommed the correct emotional reactions to them from the witnesses. I think we were correct in striking only remote spots where no damage to intelligent life…"

"First rule: We cannot harm intelligent life."

"First question: How do we know we've found some?"

"Our theory breaks down. We assumed unintelligent responses to the Black Fleet might be due to a lower order of species in remote areas, that the more intelligent might concentrate…"

"This is one of the most intense concentrations. Would you say there was any qualitative difference of intelligence in the attendant who brought us these drinks and those who witnessed our strikes in remote areas?"

"The same horror of the unknown."

"The same ability to cope with their environment barely well enough to stay alive."

"The similarities are endless. The differences are nil."

"We have not yet contacted intelligent life."

"These artifacts all around us show a high order of intelligence."

"There must be two species."

"For some reason the lower order is keeping the evidence of our visit from the knowledge of the higher order."

THEN we must make our strikes close to the areas of high order artifacts. We must smoke out the intelligent species which conceals itself."

"It may take some doing. That concealment is extraordinary. None of the individuals we have sommed acknowledge intelligence beyond their own."

"That's not the only thing we have to solve. If we are to masquerade as one of them, we've got some practice to do. They haven't negated gravity, for example. I sommed the attendant's surprise that the bed didn't sag under your weight."

"We can't afford that kind of error. If that one will detect such minor defects, think what a high order of intelligence might see."

"No more appearing as purple whirlwinds, either."

"We thought it might shock him into revealing knowledge of where the intelligent ones are to be found. That perhaps he was conspiring to conceal their presence. That perhaps they were intelligent enough to expect us and deemed it prudent to hide from us until they looked us over."

"That would be natural enough in the survival mechanism—if they were that intelligent. Surely their logic would tell them that when they started stirring in their egg it would be noticed—and investigated."

"But the attendant showed no knowledge of such a conspiracy of concealment."

"Certainly we will have to run the risk of accidentally harming intelligent life, by bringing our phenomena of visit out in the open."

"Meantime, let's practice the role of the human. Now on this matter of gravity, for example…"

"Yes, an artifact must sag when we sit on it. The carpet must show footprints when we walk on it."

"We're going to have to give over searching for the intelligent ones, at present, and concentrate on simulating the human life, instead of the intelligent one."

"For the present, then, we'll accept the most popular art form representation of humans as our model. I think we need to get out and around a bit more, get a little better idea of what is acceptable to humans. If the intelligent species is masquerading as human, he may not reveal himself to us unless we do the same. Perhaps he is concealing himself from the human, as well as from us. Perhaps he will reveal himself only when we are suitably disguised so he may reveal himself to us without, at the same time, revealing himself to the humans."

There was a murmur of agreement, and The Five merged into one invisible vortice of radiant energy. They soared through the interstices of molecules in the outer wall.

THE Night Manager, backed by the House Detective and the Dubious Bellhop, knocked discreetly on the door of 842. There was no answer. He knocked again, although his developed hotel sense already told him the room was empty, that there was no guest or intruder asleep, passed out, or refusing to answer.

He unlocked the door.

Across the room, in the far wall, he was horrified to see a three-foot spiral of radiation scorched paint. He saw a line of footprints, the carpet nap ground to a powder. He saw a deep sag, reaching almost to the floor, on this side of the bed.

These guests had been even more destructive of property than normal—and they hadn't registered, or paid, or paid their bar bill. How was that going to look on his report to management?

It was well for us that the House Detective thought this phenomenon was sufficiently outre to bring to the attention of Space Navy, Bureau of Extraterrestrial Psychology.

It was too bad that Pentagon red tape prevented the communication from reaching our department until it was too late.

Although, I still don't see what I might have done about it.

CHAPTER SEVEN

DR. KIBBIE proved right. Time was indeed precious. I had a scant month to get my program of becoming an important man into motion. Because Central Personnel was on a kick of accumulating evidence to show how much they were contributing to economy-in-government, they kept cutting my requisitions for more employees in half—and tallying up the savings to prove how efficient they were.

I endeared myself to them by doubling, tripling, quadrupling my demands, and the mushrooming numbers of people they refused to let me have would make this a banner year for them.

As it turned out, I was able to hire only two thousand five hundred and sixty-nine people and seven hundred and seventy two PhDs, in that month. My separation of the two species of employees is conscious. The PhD seems determined to separate himself from the human race; and the human race, in equal disdain, is more than agreeable. Why should I antagonize anybody through attempting to join them together again?

Once or twice Shirley did murmur some objections. Since there was more paper work involved in hiring or transferring an employee than any other employee could handle, the department had become so overburdened with handling the process that it would surely capsize and sink. I gave her the usual governmental solution to that problem: If there was too much work involved for the people in her department, then we must simply hire more people. Also, hadn't we better set up a special committee to investigate the amount of work involved?

She shuddered and pointed out that she was working night and day to administrate all this, as it was, without taking on an investigating committee. But her heart was not really in her objections, for she was able to walk the streets again without dodging former friends who played the numbers game of importance in Washington in the same way the Hollywood climber drops names.

Sara had given me no problem. When she heard I wasn't coming back to Computer Research, she took it for granted I wouldn't be able to run the government without her help.

Even Space Navy seemed a little relieved to find Sara on the scene. I was a bachelor, unattached, and Dr. Kinsey had pointed out a few things about bachelors in their late thirties. F. B. I. had not succeeded in finalizing its investigations into my secret sex practices—maybe because I hadn't had any.

Dr. Kibbie was delighted. In common with most governmental officials, he hadn't really had any idea of how enormously much two billion dollars actually is; and he wasn't sleeping well nights, worrying about how he was going to get rid of it all in time for the next appropriations. Now this seemed to be heading toward a solution. He began to bring his various department heads around to show what was being done in other yards; and they began, appropriately, to hate me.

Everything was normal—for Washington, that is.

I HADN'T really believed it, but I found my own importance was beginning to increase proportionate to the numbers of people I was hiring. Of course I was too far down the echelons to be noticed by any news reporters, to say nothing of being mentioned by any commentators; but various other minor executives were beginning to nod when we met in the halls, and even chat with me a little in the cafeteria. Guardedly, of course; and with a roving eye to make sure they were being observed by those even lower in the chain of echelon than we; and not being observed by any higher who might be inclined to place them at my level if they were seen talking to me.

Indeed, I was, at this point, still so far down in the lower levels that I hadn't felt even a remotely indirect pressure applied by one Mr. Harvey Strickland.

Of course I knew there had to be a Mr. Harvey Strickland. I had seen too many wholesome, frank, good boys, who always do what they are told, parlayed from City Councilman to the apex of government or near it in a few short years, to doubt the existence of a Harvey Strickland somewhere behind the scenes writing the script and pulling the strings.

There is always a Mr. Harvey Strickland.

This, a summary of the state of things at the time The Black Fleet struck again.

CHAPTER EIGHT

THE first announcement of the attacking Black Fleet came over the six o'clock evening analysis-of-our-troubles program. I was sitting alone in my suite at Washington's exclusive Brighton Hotel—paid for out of Dr. Kibbie's two billion as temporary quarters while my status was being clarified.

The announcement broke with stunning suddenness, in the middle of a routine analysis of the commentator's opinion of the country's opinion of the current administration as reflected in the stock market. The commentator was pausing for the Idiot's Reminder, out of camera focus, to catch up with his rapid-fire delivery, when the fax machine beside his desk suddenly went crazy.

The bell jangled urgently, the machine began to chatter and a message began to roll.

The young, scholarly commentator took one quick glance at the lead sentence. He leaped to his feet and swallowed hard. When he started to read, his voice cracked and broke. A quick witted cameraman moved in for a close-up on the fax paper; so the televiewers could read the message for themselves.

"An Air Defense Command outpost has sighted a large fleet of unidentified black, disc shaped projectiles sweeping toward the Capital from the general direction of lower Chesapeake Bay."

I cocked an eyebrow and looked at the screen sardonically. All right, so it was a government commercial telling us we should be scared enough to pay the higher taxes congress was contemplating. I could anticipate the following lines: "All citizens are urged to start digging their bomb shelters at once. The Civilian Defense Command must begin considering the appointment of regional commanders—now! Air-force antiinterceptor anti-missile anti-missile anti-missiles must receive the highest priority for research since the Black Fleet is now within a few miles of us and coming fast!"

The Black Fleet!

I gasped. It hadn't registered. Some stupe had leaked the information out of our department after all. Dr. Kibbie would be fit to be tied.

So I had failed: in my first mission—in a government of the people, by, the people, for the people—and the people were going to find out anyhow.

There had been a longer than normal pause while the commentator kept looking off to one side. He turned back to face the audience.

"We take you now to our own Bobby Lovelace, news analyst directly at the scene," he informed us.

"Oh sure," I said, in disgust. "Ham it up boys. Long as you've let it out, milk it for everything it's got."

There was the usual flickering on the screen and a new face appeared. No doubt their own Bobby Lovelace. His eyes were distended, his face pale; his hands trembled.

"Evil!" he was mouthing in a whisper. "Horrible! Unclean! You'll see when they get there. I can't talk about it. You'll see for yourselves." He waved his hands in negation before his face. The camera moved off him and the screen blanked out.

"Oh come now, fellows," I exclaimed aloud. "That's hamming it up too much. Even for television."

BUT my skepticism was jarred when, from far down Connecticut Avenue, there drifted the faint, strange sound of a pulsating siren. Nearby, police whistles begin to shrill, stop, shrill again, stop, shrill again—the best that could be accomplished on short notice to sound an air raid warning.

"This is going pretty far," I murmured.

But it must have had its effect on some, for in the adjoining suite the sounds of a cocktail party for some petty senator faded to a strangled, waiting silence.

For the first time, I felt unease; as if there were something in the atmosphere.

"Good God," I breathed. "Don't tell me that even I am responding to such Hollywood hokum!"

The screen came on again, and we were back in the Washington studio. The young commentator, whose face still reflected his first shock, had had a little time to collect himself; but he had to try three times before he could light a nonchalant cigarette. The cameraman must have been assigned an acting part, also, because he was having trouble keeping the news desk and fax machine in focus.

The fax machine was still. And that stillness was even more compelling than its frantic activity had been.

"They've put a good director on this production," I said, still aloud. "I think I'll watch it—might turn into a pretty good show after all."

And then, to my astonishment, I was beginning to wonder if it were staged, after all. Perhaps it was the tenseness in the atmosphere. The air was heavy, stifling. I got up out of my chair and walked across the room to open the french windows which let out upon a private balcony. There were no street noises. In this neighborhood it was always quiet, subdued in the genteel manner; but there was always that distant throb of a city inhabited by people who were more than one quarter alive. Now there seemed to be a sound vacuum.

I walked back and sat down again before the television.

The commentator picked up a sheet of his script, looked at it with an air of wonderment, then he raised his eyes to the camera again.

115

"Well," he said simply. "I guess we'll just have to wait this out together."

I caught myself nodding in agreement.

"Good work," I said approvingly. "Damn good work." But somehow, now, my persistence in regarding it as fiction seemed the tawdry unreality, instead of, as usual, the production.

We waited it out together.

I began to wonder if I should try to get down to my office at the Pentagon, but checked the impulse by asking what I would do after I got there. If this did prove fiction, that kind of response could make any official a laughing stock. If it were not fiction…

I swallowed.

I LOOKED at the commentator again. He was still sitting. He shrugged. He looked down at his script. He looked up again. He flicked the script he had been reading before the announcement.

"Seems silly to go on with this drivel, now," he said.

I think that blasphemous statement convinced me more than anything else. That, and nothing happening. For the first law of entertainment is that something must be happening every minute, every second.

Outside, another siren began to take up the wail.

The fax machine started to chatter again. Now the commentator was able to read the message as it appeared. His voice was clear, but tense.

"Bulletin…London… Unknown projectiles in large numbers are approaching up the Thames from the Channel Coast.

…

"Bulletin…Tokyo… Missiles maneuvering at high altitudes near Yokahama…

"Bulletin…Moscow… Antimissile missiles released against enemy projectiles…last warning to United States…call off attack…or we will press button…

"Bulletin…Omaha…last warning to Russia…call off attack or we will press button…

The machine stopped abruptly. The commentator stared at it, uncomprehending.

After a few seconds it chattered out another very brief message. "Projectiles now over Washington."

I stood up, uncertain, dazed, pondering the habit of getting my information from the screen versus going to see for myself. As if coming out of sleep I shook off the stupidity and, in a kind of reluctance, forced myself to walk over to the french windows and out upon the balcony.

The July dusk had blended into night. Stars were clear and bright in the moonless sky. Street lights had been shut off in accord with some dusty, moulded plan of the past, but at the distant shopping center a neon glow suggested store owners hadn't been told about it; or maybe they were straining for one last sale before being blown to Kingdom Come.

Over downtown Washington, some eight miles to the Southeast, a weird, red haze was forming in the sky. Swiftly it swelled, and grew, and took shape; with formations of tongues of flame. And now the whole sky was a mass of red, leaping flames.

Out of the flames, as if against a backdrop on a stage, there silhouetted the dead black discs.

My gorge rose in revulsion, I fought for detachment; to still my atavistic fears; to remind myself that man had created the dread forces of Evil out of his own sick imaginings, even as he had created the forces of Good out of his noble aspirations. It did no good. This was materialization of something basically, inherently Evil, no sickness of the imagination.

Something seemed to go awry with my time sense. I seemed suspended in a kind of time vacuum, a new realization of how much we depend upon it for the sense of continuity. I could not tell whether things were happening simultaneously, instantaneously, or with long lapses of time in between.

THE discs were maneuvering now at dazzling speed, sharply wheeling in one direction, veering with incredible violation of momentum's laws in another. Breaking, scattering, one moment in quantum particle randomness; the next in circle, in boxed, or V, or straight line formation; obeying some principle pattern all their own, without meaning to me, to us, to man.

From the Earth crimson fingers of anti-aircraft fire reached up for the projectiles.

The night was slashed into flaming, criss-cross patterns of white and red tracer missile lines. But I saw no disc hesitate, falter, fall. At times of randomness some seemed hurtling toward Earth; and yet a second, (a moment? an hour?) later, when they flashed into some unexpected formation, none were laggard from wounds, none a hairsbreadth out of line.

Perhaps our barrage was missing its target entirely, perhaps deflected by some force we could not know, perhaps passing through without harm. Who could know?

At times, some single disc, plunging downward toward me, toward us all, with crushing speed, and sending me cowering back against the window frame, seemed almost to fill the whole sky, incredibly huge, incomprehensibly massive; yet later (how much later?) no more than a black pinpoint against the flaming yellow and crimson sky. For they were maneuvering in depth as well as across the vault of our sky—in third dimension. And, for all we knew, in some mathematical fourth, as well?

For surely no power on Earth had a science which could violate the laws of inertia with such impunity. And if not of Earth, then what Earthly logic could we calculate to apply?

We ceased streaking our futile anti-missile missiles at them now. The discs dominated the sky, alone.

And then, as if man were realizing in that peril that the human brain might, after all, creatively function on the spur of the moment to prove superior to the planned patterns of mechanical brains, and with some antiquated tools at hand prove yet superior to modern instruments; Air Force interceptors came up and into the sky.

As if to complement their tiny V, the discs formed a mighty V to stretch across the sky. I felt a sob quicken my throat, admiration of such incredible bravery; shame that I was sometimes sardonic and cynical of man.

"Dammit," I heard myself saying over and over. "Dammit, dammit." That such courage should be so futile.

THE blur of my grief for man streaked the lights. The clutches of wing missiles soared out ahead of the interceptors, the sonic booms shocked and roared and made puny the sounds of firing. Puny, too, the little V as it approached the apex of the gigantic one, but dammit, how brave!

The points of the tiny and the great merged. Our small was lost in the huge, swallowed in flaming radiance.

But when the vast V wheeled away, majestically, the interceptors could be discerned once more; yes, there they were, zooming wildly, as if out of control, into space.

Yet not out of control, no. I felt my caught breath return, hurting, when I saw them reforming into attack groups. Section by trained section they peeled off, in traditional patterns preserved out of a long dead past, they hurled in sonic booming speeds toward the giant V. Small groups of us, attacking theirs, them. At the sides of their apex instead of its point, cutting loose at them with near numbing barrages, and using the very forces of recoil to pull the interceptors up and out of their screaming power dives.

And against all our unleashed might, not one single projectile wavered from the huge formation.

Crouched there on the balcony, my back cowering against the solid window frame, the only seeming solid thing in a boiling fluid world of noise and motion and light, I watched the fight go on.

The fight?

There was no fight. There was Man, spewing all his power, all his might, all the fierce, aggressive product of his brain and hand against his enemy. How had we known it enemy?

But there was no fight.

For the discs were not striking back. No red ray coruscated down and down to melt our City into flowing stone.

My senses numbed.

There had been not even falling shrapnel, broken pieces of missiles fired from our own at them. It was as if some unknown vacuum cleaner, electro-magnet, sucked up the debris of battle as it occurred—to keep our people safe and our streets clean.

Spent interceptors returned to Earth, new waves of others arose to take their place—no less brave, no less determined.

IGNORED now by the discs, they spent themselves in turn.

The great V no longer paid us the compliment of wheeling massively to meet our charge. Rather now it seemed bent on some purpose of its own, without regard.

Yes, the farther ends of the angle lines were curving inward bending, bending inward until at last they met. A cloudiness appeared in circle at the center, and at its center an incredibly bright spot of pure crimson light. The cloudy haze coalesced, solidified, striated.

A monstrous, pupil pierced and piercing, bloodshot eye looked down upon the city.

I later learned it was the common experience of each human being in the city, but at that moment was convinced the piercing gaze seemed directed upon me into me, through, me.

The eye, at first stretching almost from horizon, to horizon, was smaller now. Now it filled but half the sky. And this before I had realized it was shrinking at all, so firm its hypnotic gaze. But now that I had realized it, the shrinking was accelerated; the eye was going away from us; out into space.

Yet even to the last, that piercing pupil penetrated me, impaled me upon its malevolent beam of light.

And then it, too, winked out.

The flaming mists of the sky cleared. In the distance, over Rock Creek Park, I could see the last interceptors returning to Earth.

There seemed no triumph in their flight.

The sky was clear and black. The stars shone bright—and cold. No longer friendly stars, twinkling the planets at us as if with amusement at the foibles of man.

No longer friendly sky, velvet soft and comforting.

There were Things out there. Our tiny Earth was spinning through that cold, remorseless vacuum, alone.

And nothing to hide behind.

CHAPTER NINE

FOR three days the Black Fleet appeared, and disappeared, and reappeared. Over every major city of the Earth. The Black Fleet? The many, many Black Fleets. So often, simultaneously, in so many places that the wildest sort of reckoning could not estimate their number.

Now there was no thought of nation against nation, man against man; man taming other men to his service, submission, his pattern of the only Right.

Now the discs had reappeared over New York City once more. But this time their pattern was different. They did not appear, play out their ominous and meaningless formations, wash the Earth below them in a stinking miasma of revolting, evil dread; and then to disappear.

They stayed. For seven hours now they had hovered and circled endlessly; as if they waited for momentous signal known only to them.

The city below seemed virtually dead. On appearance, at noon this time, having seen them several times before, the New Yorker had cocked an eye heavenward, shrugged and gone about his business. But the fleet had stayed, and as if somewhere a valve had been opened to let off the steam, the city slowed, and died.

No one knew where or how it started, but through the long afternoon the feeling grew universal that this time they meant business. This was it. And the waiting grew intolerable.

The waiting grew intolerable for Mr. Harvey Strickland.

He sat, robed in his purple dressing gown, on his high backed and carved throne chair, there in his penthouse, atop one of his many newspaper buildings. He watched the television wall, and curled his lip in fury.

It wasn't going over. With his expert, uncanny feel of mass reaction, he knew his organization was missing fire. They went through the motions of the formula, but too many of them were

"For three days the Black Fleet appeared, disappeared and reappeared. Over every major city of the Earth. So often, simultaneously, in so many places that the wildest sort of reckoning could not possibly estimate their number."

like that first announcer of the projectiles. Too many of them considered the stuff they spoke and printed as mere drivel. He'd fired the guy, of course, for letting the public see that he considered it so much nonsense, and ordinarily this would have been enough to make the rest of his organization men dig in with added display of enthusiasm, smacking their lips to show how much they enjoyed eating the crap. But they weren't.

And the people weren't buying the crap.

Instead of watching his television screens and reading his newspapers for their interpretation, the damn people were seeing for themselves!

His radio and television channels were blanketed with Harvey Strickland's own subsidized exhorters who pled, stormed, raged and threatened the people to get down on their knees, bow their heads in humility.

His scornful lip lifted from his lengthened, yellowed teeth. Humility! He knew it, the Harvey Stricklands had always known that humility was the basest, most ignoble, unworthy posture a man can find; but it was the formula which had brought man back to groveling in the dust again and again. Subservient to the Harvey Stricklands, serving their ends.

The formula just wasn't going over!

The rabbits sat in their warrens and cowered from the hunters above them—and the hunters, this time, were not controlled by Harvey Strickland. There should be line up and clamor for self-destruction.

HE pushed his massive body, groaning under the weight of fat, out of his throne chair and began to pace the floor in sudden fury. Dammit, he'd missed his cue. He should have set up a scapegoat, a whole bunch of scapegoats. He should have manufactured some victims for the majority to persecute. Hell, that was the simplest formula in the book. With just a little twist of words, any minority group could be made to look responsible for the Black Fleet. It always worked.

And he'd slipped on it.

He knew damn well humans would never go out and tackle anything stronger than they were. They had to feel they were in the majority. Oh they were strong on crusading for perfectly safe subjects, these humans; but they had to have something weak and running in fear before they'd change over from rabbits to dogs and run baying after it in furious, frenzied chase.

But, dammit, he hadn't had time. Nobody had tipped him off to expect the Black Fleet. What was the matter with that Pentagon? Why hadn't they tipped him off? Wasn't it their business to know, to anticipate? And weren't they completely dependent upon him to shape the mass mind for them?

And why hadn't his own direct organization men been on their toes, and even without warning, put the formula into motion without waiting to be told? Hell, he'd trained them well enough. They'd been pampered and spoiled with the high wages he paid them, the silly little status levels he'd granted them, to the point that they would sacrifice anything, anything at all to keep their position. That was his technique. He'd seen to it that all his independent editors, on both side of every fence, said what he wanted them to say: the pro faction coming out strong, the con faction advancing such weak arguments against that even a child could see the only possible right way to look at the question. Every damn one of his free and fearless commentators and columnists said exactly what he wanted them to say. They didn't get hired unless their past opinions showed they could be trusted. They didn't work for him if they didn't go on freely and independently coming to the conclusions favorable to Mr. Harvey Strickland. Hell, they couldn't work anywhere if they didn't do that.

So now in a real emergency, they'd sat on their overstuffed duffs and let the Black Fleet take over without making one move to capitalize on it to strengthen his position.

ANGRILY, he waddled over to the television monitors, and flipped the switch to turn them off—a symbolic destruction of them all. He turned to do the same thing to the battery of fax machines lined up along the wall, but paused to read the latest messages.

The same thing was happening everywhere, over all the large cities of America, over every large city in the world.

Everywhere, the discs hovered, and wheeled in formation, and waited.

An unbidden doubt tried to force its way into his mind that there might be no opportunity in this to tighten his hold on the mass mind still more; that this might be something beyond his capacity to turn to his own advantage. He shook his massive head angrily, and shrugged off the weakness. He would not allow such an idea to take full form in his mind. He would be no better than the damn rabbits he despised if he did.

But there could be no doubt about one thing. The Black Fleet was getting ready for the kill. And he didn't see one single angle for getting in on the winning end of it, somehow.

If there were only some way he could get next to the projectiles, deal with them. They must want something. There must be minds inside those discs. And where there were minds capable of all this, there were also minds capable of working the angles. Capable of dominating the whole Earth in three days, as these were, they should also be capable of recognizing one of their own, and his right to be in the pot—himself, accustomed to dominating, one Harvey Strickland.

So if they wanted to dominate the Earth, why didn't they deal?

Why weren't they putting out feelers?

A new thought crept in to horrify him. What if they had been doing just that? Hell, they could have taken over that first night. So what else could be the meaning of all that pointless appearing and reappearing? What if they were hovering there now, from noon until near dusk, waiting, waiting for him to respond to their feelers?

And he didn't know how?

The frustration, exasperation pumped powerful shots of adrenalin into his blood, made him forget to wheeze and groan in protest against gravity pulling at his fat. His rage sent him waddling, almost running, out to the garden surrounding his house on top of the building. He watched the fading sky, followed the projectiles— as if by the very power of his eyes he could make them take notice of him, come to him, deal with him.

They wanted to control the people, didn't they? They hadn't killed any of them off, so they must want them preserved for some end. Well, he controlled the people. He owned 'em. They'd have to come to him in the long run.

Or did they figure to just highjack the lot of them, right out from under him?

UP there among the circling, black discs, there wasn't a single anti-missile missile; not one. Not even a damn interceptor. There wasn't any sound of anti-aircraft fire. They'd given up trying to fight. When it was all over, the people would clean up the mess, and hope. He snorted in disgust as his mind gave him the picture of the terrible and futile patience of people who can't do anything but try—and hope.

Dammit! Why didn't his phone ring? He'd put in another call to Washington. Why didn't the operator get him through?

The heat of his anger, the residual heat of the day even at this height of a hundred stories up, made him loosen the purple robe which swathed his rolls of fat. He walked over to the parapet surrounding his penthouse garden and looked out over it, a hundred stories below. But the damn ants weren't crawling around on the threads of streets to amuse him as usual. There, to one side, the East River was a silver ribbon that partly encircled Manhattan. He had once thought of it as a silver ribbon around a tinseled Christmas package—all for him.

Above him arose the transmitter tower of one of his New York television stations. It was a symbol, too, a royal scepter, if you please; more powerful and more commanding of subjugation of men's minds than that of any king who ever lived. The sight of it, still standing there, pointed at the projectiles as an accusing finger points at God, telling him to mind his manners and do as he is told or the people will dismiss him as casually as they have dismissed so many other gods in the past, the sight of it restored his calm, his confidence of his power and destiny.

He looked at the projectiles again, and this time calculatingly, with detachment. Let them send out their feelers he didn't know how to answer. Let them strike, let them dominate, let them take control of Earth. In the long run they'd have to come to him. Because you can't control the actions of men unless you control their minds.

He chuckled sardonically. Every conqueror in the past had

found out the same thing: You can't control a country without help from the people, some people, of that country. So when these conquerors tried to take over, and work through the men already established, they'd find out something. Something Harvey Strickland already knew: That when a man sells his independence of thought for money or status, without realizing it he also sells his capacity for independence of thought; and like the worn-out columnists and commentators he must play the same old record over and over, because he has no capacity for taking a fresh point of view.

All through the whole structure there were men who had sold out to him; and when these conquerors tried to use those men, they'd have to turn to him.

Yes whoever was back of these projectiles would have to come to him in the end. He looked up at them, still hovering above. He laughed loudly again, then turned confidently and waddled back through the french doors, which led from the garden to his office.

AT his desk he sat down heavily, picked up the phone, and grinned in visioning the instant apprehension of the man on the switchboard down in the bowels of the building.

"Got that call through yet?" he demanded.

"N-n-no, s-sir," the man stammered.

"Quit chittering. Why haven't you got Higgins?"

"Well, sir, his staff says that since he is Senate majority leader he is in a big meeting at the White House, with the general staff, and they won't..."

"Oh, shut up. Gimme the Washington operator, one with some authority."

"Supervisor," a voice chimed into the receiver.

"This is Harvey Strickland," he said. "Break a circuit and put me through to the White House."

There was a very short delay.

"Yes, Mr. Strickland," she came back on the line with the words. "Right away."

Almost immediately the White House switchboard answered.

"This is Harvey Strickland," he said again. "Get Senator Higgins on the phone for me."

"He is in a meeting with the President, the Cabinet, the General Staff, and the Heads of the Department of Extraterrestrial Psychology…" she began.

"I said this was Harvey Strickland," he enunciated slowly, ominously.

"Yes, sir. I know who you are, sir," she said. Then doubtfully, "I'll see, sir."

He shifted angrily in his chair. Someone would pay for this inconvenience.

"This, is Tom Higgins, Harvey," a voice came through.

"Well, how about it?" Strickland demanded.

"No decision yet, Harvey," the Senate Majority Leader answered apologetically.

"What! Why, dammit, what're you guys doing down there? You go back to that meeting and tell them to use an H-Bomb on those projectiles and no more nonsense about it. Dammit, Higgins, you hear me?"

Tom Higgins voice drifted to him then, old and weary.

"Yeah, Harvey, I hear you."

"Well then, get back in there and goose them pinhead generals off their fat duffs!"

"THERE are a lot of angles to this thing, Harvey." Higgins' voice seemed to grow stronger.

"We've got a couple of experts on extraterrestrial psychology testifying. A Doctor Kibbie and a Doctor Ralph Kennedy. Kibbie doesn't know anything, he's just a promoter. But Kennedy talks some sense. He says there's something odd and peculiar about the behavior pattern. I don't know, he says a lot of things, but he does point out one thing you can't get around, Harvey. They haven't hurt us yet. That's an angle, you know."

"Angles!" Strickland shouted. His voice was high and shrill. "Don't give me any stuff about angles. Don't give me any of that professor talk about peculiar patterns of behavior. I know what the angle is. I know what they're waiting for. They're waiting to hear from me. That's what this is all about. And I'm gonna give 'em an answer. The answer is gonna be the H-Bomb. They're gonna find out I got a little trick or so of my own. Drop that damn H-Bomb on them. That's all I want."

"Look, Harvey," Higgins tried to reason with him, "The discs are over big cities. A whole city would be wiped out—a million people or more."

"'Who cares?"

"Well, now, Harvey...public opinion..."

"Public opinion? For Chrissake, who you think tells the public what its opinion is? Dammit, Tom, gimme a week with my newspapers and my television and radio stations—and you've got any kind of public opinion you want to ask for. You know that. You know how you've been elected all these terms. And if the President has forgotten..."

"But all those innocent people..." Higgins said, almost with a groan.

"All those innocent people," Strickland mimicked. "So what'll happen? Hell. You know what it'll do, well as me. It always does it, any kind of trouble. It sends 'em back to their beds to breed faster, to make even more people than was lost. Far as opinion goes, them that don't get hit will shrug it off. They weren't hurt, so why squawk. Them what do get hit won't matter. Look Tom, you gotta take the broad view of these things. You tell them generals to stop shillyshallying around, listening to college professors, and get back to doing what they're suppose to do. Drop that H-Bomb, and stop arguing."

"Okay, Harvey," Higgins answered faintly. "I'll tell them how you feel."

"Whoa! Back up! It doesn't make any difference how I feel. See? I'm just a newspaper man. I just print the news. I don't make it. I got to tell you this again? Something you learned thirty years ago?"

"But Harvey! Something as big as this. They won't drop the H-Bomb on my sayso. Something big as this, Harvey, maybe you've got to come out into the open..."

"And if I do, how'm I going to mold public opinion? I'd be an interested party. And if I can't mold public opinion, you'll all go down the drain."

"Maybe we should, Harvey. Maybe we should."

"Now you look here, Tom," Harvey Strickland took a negotiating tone. "This is not your decision to make. You're not a military man. You're not trained to make the kind of decisions a military man has to make. So it won't be your decision. It'll be their decision. All you have to do is remind them they're military men.

"Remind them to go back and pick up on their West Point training, and places like that. Remind them to stop thinking about people and start thinking about troops and forces. Troops and forces don't bleed, you know. They're just tactical problems on blackboards.

"Remind them about those conversations they used to have; where they used to speculate on whether the lower orders actually had any nerves and feelings. And the lower orders being anybody who didn't go to West Point, or the like. If they've developed weak stomachs, tell them to start thinking about maps and forces and calculated risks, the way they were trained. Hell, they're trained to be killers, so what's stopping them?

"You understand me, Tom?"

"I'll tell them, Harvey," the voice sounded sick.

"Yeah," Strickland said contemptuously. "I thought you would."

HE put down the receiver and rubbed his hands together. He didn't resent having to blow some steam into his men once in a while. It was a reminder of what they would be without him.

They wouldn't decide to use New York as the test city, of course. Because he was in New York.

And they wouldn't decide to use Washington, because they were in Washington.

It would be some place like St. Louis, maybe. There'd been a strong, unaccountable anti-vote in St. Louis last election. Maybe he'd better give some more thought to replacing some editors and station managers out there. Then he chuckled. He was forgetting. There wouldn't be any to replace after a few minutes. If they decided on St. Louis. Maybe he'd better call Tom and tell him to use St. Louis. No, better not. Let them make the decision.

He touched a button beside one of the jeweled lights along the ledge of his desk; and knew it was like touching a raw nerve to make the man at the other end jump out of his chair and start running to the elevator. All these buttons were nerve endings, the nerves reaching down through the executive offices from penthouse to basement, even down to the sub basement where giant presses thundered day and night to grind out read-and-repeat public opinion.

Precisely in the number of seconds it would take for his secretary to rush from his office, give the special signal to the elevator reserved for express trips to the penthouse, and the operator to make the pickup and full speed to the top, the elevator door in one wall of his office opened. From the door there stepped a gray, gaunt man who walked resolutely across the wide expanse of floor between the elevator and the desk.

This was Miller, Strickland's personal secretary.

Forty years ago, Miller had been a college hero, the most popular man on the campus, the president of the senior class, the president of the united fraternity council. That class had also contained one Harvey Strickland, not a college hero, virtually unknown on the campus, and president of nothing.

Miller had been the man voted most likely to, succeed. Strickland had received one vote—his own. But he had known, even then, that his vote counted more than all the rest.

The friendless hours of Strickland's college years were not lonely. He was busy accumulating information about each of his classmates, their families, their friends.

The dossiers grew thick with facts and notes. They contained the essence of every chance contact he made. They contained records of invitations not issued to him and the refusals of his. They contained details of the contemptuous refusals of girls. They contained every honor each classmate had received. And every honor which he himself, had not received was an insult to be revenged—someday.

The dossier of Miller was thickest of them all.

Oh, that senior class scattered after graduation, like a flock of giddy butterflies. He could not keep track of them all, and in later years it had cost him a fortune in detective agency fees to trace them all. A fortune well spent.

HE had had one advantage over them. They'd ridden, sheltered and in comfort, on society's protection-of-youth train. They expected, to go on riding, in equal shelter and comfort. They knew nothing else. But he had had to slog it out, step by weary step, all the way. He knew the score, and began to cash in on it long before they began to get the hint that there even was a score. And that it wasn't added up the way their professors thought.

Lost in the melee of living in an adult world, fully realized only by him, was a certain statistic. For some odd reason, only one man in that senior class had succeeded in life. For everyone else, after the first few years of promising bright success, everything seemed to go wrong. Whatever they grasped seemed somehow to turn into dust in their fingers. They never knew why.

Other men, lesser men, might have been tempted to let them know the prime mover behind the scenes, remind them of the cuts and slights and indifference, remind them they had backed the wrong horse, ignored the right one. This was not the Strickland way. This was the most delicious part of his triumph; that they never knew why. To believe that their failure was their own inadequacy was the deeper satisfaction; for if they had known their failure was not their own doing their self-respect might have been preserved.

This was the real power of secret rule through secret dossier, established as governmental and industrial policy a hundred years before. This was the source of his indescribable pleasure indefinitely prolonged; to take the place of wife, children, home, friendship.

He looked now at Miller, gaunt and gray, over sixty, standing there before him, a clerk-servant, patiently waiting to be instructed, apparently beaten and resigned. The man should be happy to have this job at all. It was the first one he had been able to hold for more than a few months in all those forty years since school. He should be glad to have found a haven at last, where he could get the same paternal protection on which he had grown dependent in those years in a psycho ward; where the psychiatrists had finally convinced him to accept and adjust to the idea that he simply didn't have the stuff of success within him. That being a college hero had been only a fluke of adolescent misjudgment, based in nothing more than a handsome face, a charming personality, and the backing of once wealthy parents. Parents who unaccountably lost all their money, and position, and never knew why.

IT did not occur to Strickland, then, that his contempt for Miller had, on occasion, made him underestimate the man; that more than once Miller had stood patiently at his elbow while he worked the combination of the vault which held all those secret dossiers. That as his personal secretary, Miller knew his movements so well that he knew when it was safe for him to work the combination he had seen and memorized, enabling him to find out why.

Strickland let him stand, a moment longer, passively; then dictated an announcement to him that the government was about to take dramatic action against the enemy. Then as an afterthought, he added, "Have the agency compile the usual data on a Dr. Ralph Kennedy, some damn title like Extraterrestrial Psychologist. The agency can find him. He's big enough to be invited to the White House for consultation on the psychology of the enemy. He gave me some trouble. Damn near had the general staff convinced they ought to wait until the enemy... Never mind, just tell the agency to get on it."

He waved a negligent hand then, and Miller walked back to the elevator, which was waiting for him in the floor below, out of earshot but handy. Strickland turned to the fax machine and began watching the sweep hand of the clock to see how many seconds it would take for the announcement to show.

It hit the special bulletin to all communication mediums machine when it should. Regardless of what might be going on elsewhere, his machine was still functioning as it should. It backed up his confidence that even if the rest of the country, the rest of the world, was going to the dogs; he was still in position to grind out the easy to repeat slogans, which would jell into public opinion, made to order.

Less than two minutes after reading his bulletin on the fax machine that the government was going to get off the dime and act, Higgins' call came through from Washington.

"Okay, Harvey," Higgins said in a voice which seemed drained of all life. "They made the decision you want. They're going to put H-Bomb warheads on some anti-missile missiles. They've got 'em stored in ordnance depots around, labeled 'Experimental Explosives'. That's so the local commands won't guess what they really are, panic, and try to get out. They couldn't decide which city to use first. The President made the decision. I expect he remembers the way the last vote went. He's got that kind of mind. So it's St. Louis.

"If we fail there, then next is Detroit; then Toledo; then Dallas. God have mercy on us all. God have mercy on you, Harvey...and on me." The voice trailed away.

"Splendid, Tom," Strickland said heartily. "You always deliver. I'll personally watch it on my television monitors."

If the Senate Majority Leader appreciated this special consideration he was getting, he didn't acknowledge it.

HE turned to the network monitor to watch St. Louis go out in a blaze of glory, hoping to catch a glimpse of the actual explosion before the screen would go blank and dead. Instead of St. Louis, he saw one of his pantywaist announcers driveling along about the formations over New York, as if that were important.

He felt a quick surge of anger until he realized the network couldn't know something was going to happen over St. Louis. He pulled the phone toward him, to tell the network to switch over to St. Louis; but an afterthought made him pull his hand away without lifting the receiver. Just in case, just in case there ever was enough opposition to amount to anything, and just in case some treacherous traitor in his own outfit told them he'd switched them over to St. Louis before the explosion...before, meaning he'd known in advance...

He would have to deny himself the pleasure of watching his orders carried out.

Never mind there was another way. There'd have to be some kind of communication between the projectiles. Those circling overhead would know their St. Louis formation had been wiped out. They'd go streaking west to concentrate on the attack. That would tell him, just as well.

He wanted to go out to his roof garden again, to be watching them at the instant they heard; see their confusion, see them go. But he also wanted to stay by his fax machines and television monitors because Kansas City, maybe as far away as Des Moines, they'd pick up the explosion and report it.

The conflict of desires made him furious and he pounded on his desk in frustration that he couldn't be both places at the same time.

The minutes ticked slowly away. The fax machines were still reporting nothing beyond the paralysis of the big cities, the fear, the foreboding, the total helplessness.

Dammit! Why did the military have to be so slow? Them and their red tape! Now if it was under his control—if it was his organization, St. Louis would have been destroyed in five minutes and his stupid minions would be back clicking their heels and asking what he wanted now, sir. But the stinking military. He thought of the handsome, lean, virile young officers. He turned livid with rage. Handsome, lean and virile he had never been.

And then he chuckled softly. There would be handsome, lean and virile ones manning their stations at St. Louis. They would be putting Explosive X in their missiles, not knowing, never knowing, that in another instant they would be handsome, lean and virile no longer.

It was fully dark out now. Here in New York. It would still be light in St. Louis, but it was dark here. There was a red glow around the discs, but nothing like the flaming skies of the first night.

Twenty minutes passed, then one of the fax machines began to jangle loudly, to call attention to the special news, as distinct from filler stuff.

It would be the far machine to make him get up from his desk!

But it was date lined, St. Louis! That couldn't be!

The message rolled out before him. The local anti-air attack services had decided to try a secret explosive not yet tried against the projectiles. But the anti-missile missiles had failed to function. There was no accounting for it. They just didn't function. Not one would fire.

The X Explosive was being loaded into interceptor jets. It would be taken by human pilots directly into the formation of the enemy and released. Upon request of their commanders, suicide volunteers had stepped forward to the last man.

The machine fell silent.

STRICKLAND sighed in relief. So that was the reason for the delay. Well, it simply prolonged the pleasure of anticipation. He'd look at it that way. The suicide boys would do the job. Too bad there hadn't been time for his local organization to get television cameras on the scene.

More minutes passed. He remained standing at the machine. He didn't really expect it to register another message. How could it, when the H-Bomb let go? But another city, on this or some other machine, depending on which line was clear. He waited. Still more minutes passed.

The machine jangled again. And again date lined St. Louis.

"Interceptors return to base. –30—"

"What do you mean, end of message?" Strickland roared. "To hell with it...you're fired out there, whoever you are!"

But another machine began to jangle, and pulled him away from the silent one. Detroit was reporting the same failure of missiles to fire. The same suicide pilots to take the X Explosive to the enemy. Then the same silence, the same waiting.

And the same report that the interceptors had returned to base. But this reporter, apparently more enterprising, gave out with more.

The pilots were obviously out of their minds.

"I couldn't trip the release," one of them was babbling, according to the fax machine. "The automatics wouldn't function on proximity. I didn't bring her back. She brought me back. Something took over the controls of the ship. I didn't land her, she landed me."

In sheer fury, Strickland kicked the machine, and tears formed in his eyes at the hurt to his foot.

Sheer funk it was. Sheer yellow funk! Damn! What an investigation this would make when it was all over!

A moment to sober his mood. A moment's thought.

The mind in the projectiles hadn't let him respond to their feelers! They hadn't let him wipe out a few of their ships, just to show them he could do it. They weren't opening negotiations with him. They didn't play the game according to the human rules. If he were willing to sacrifice a million or so of his own pawns, they should have been willing to sacrifice theirs. That was the way the game was always played before the big boys got down to serious business of dividing up the pot.

For the first time he allowed the doubt to take form. The doubt that they might need him, after all.

His contemplation was interrupted by a clear, piercing note. It was like a trumpet; no, more like a bugle call. It came through the french windows. It flooded the room with its warm, golden sound. He whirled away from the fax machines and rushed to the garden outside.

The last, lingering notes seemed to flood the whole city.

HE stumbled out to the edge of the garden, to lean against the parapet while he gazed up into the heavens.

There were the projectiles, seeming to draw together now. But high above them, apparently so high they still caught the light from the sun below his horizon, a new set of ships had appeared. Each an iridescent globe. They flew in a wing formation, a vast wing. It was like a wing of shining pearls.

They came closer. They began to shade into iridescent blue.

And like the star sapphire, even at this distance he could see the symbol on each of them—a shining white cross of radiant light.

CHAPTER TEN

JUST before the trumpet flooded Washington with golden sound, we were on our way home from the White House conference. The plan was for the Space Cadet driving our staff car to drop Sara off at the building where she shared an apartment with Shirley, then to leave me at my hotel.

The summons to the White House conference had hit me with

a gulping surprise. It shouldn't have. For three days now, and a good share of the hours in the two nights, our department in the Pentagon had been swarming with brass and braid trying to get a line on the psychology of our enemy. Which was natural enough, since that was supposed to be our job.

Dr. Kibbie was a bitter disappointment. He plain funked it. There was no other interpretation. On that first morning, after the evening strike, it became abundantly clear to me that in spite of all his talk about the rumors of the Black Fleet, he hadn't really believed in it—that he merely used the rumors to further his con game.

The other department heads in the Bureau of Extraterrestrial Psychology responded characteristically. In common with government bureau heads generally they could talk learnedly about the problem so long as it was kept at a distance, but displayed a complete helplessness to cope when it pushed its reality into our faces.

Somehow, without intending it, I found myself covering up for them, rationalizing their vagueness into something which sounded at least remotely sensible, taking on the burdens of soothing irate and insistent generals and admirals which Kibbie and his other department heads were shunting in my direction. Without intending it, I was rapidly becoming the answer-boy. Only I didn't have any solid answers, either.

Word had got around about my previous dealings with psychological oddities. This seemed to make me an authority on alien psychology. Perhaps the experiences had helped. Perhaps, without realizing it, I actually had developed—well, if not an open mind, one, which was at least cracked.

DR. Gerald Gaffey, Harvard's gift to the science of vocational guidance for extraterrestrials turned out to be astonishingly useful. He was surprisingly adept at speculative extrapolation. He proved a valuable assistant because he had the capacity for picking up the vaguest speculation, expanding it and rationalizing it until it made sense.

That he was probably quite wrong was in itself an asset. The human mind, somehow, seems much more attracted by the false than by the true; and, being wrong, therefore, we were able to satisfy the brass and braid, and send them on their happy way.

Being wrong in so many ways assisted me in another respect. Since the wrong answers differed so widely in their substance that they couldn't all be the right wrong, I began to doubt the rightness of any of the wrongs. A little more time and I would have begun to doubt the reality of the ominous discs overhead at all.

It was in this mood that I talked at the White House conference. There, in that sound proofed room, presumably not bugged by more than a half dozen foreign powers, although certainly bugged by our own secret services who would record each word spoken and try to confound its author twenty years later if he began to give trouble, the reality of the maneuvering discs overhead seemed less believable; and the smell of their Evil seemed not to penetrate.

I had almost convinced the general staff and the President that since we hadn't yet been hurt, only frightened, and didn't really know these things were our enemy perhaps our best course was to do more sampling, collating and correlating of statistics, to learn more about them—particularly since we had already shot everything except our ultimate weapon against them without effect.

It was then that Senator Higgins had been called out of the conference. When he came back, I could see at once that I had lost. With a few terse words, spoken through grim lips which hardly moved, he pointed out that the enemy discs were hovering over every major city of the world, that they were in a position to strike the killing blow without giving us the chance to defend ourselves; and that it was the height of irresponsible cowardice to wait until they had done it.

IT was the semantics of "cowardice", of course, which turned the tide. Better-to-be-cautious-and-alive-than-brave-and-dead was not a concept of speculative extrapolation comfortable to the military mind. The President, after a shrewd look at Higgins, and an apparently correct interpretation of the message he read in the Senator's sick eyes, switched polarity with the practiced ease of a winning politician, and added his argument that it was time America recaptured its leadership of the world, that other nations were faltering in the face of duty, and that once more we had opportunity to be First.

I was preemptorly dismissed with the implication that in the face of all this opportunity I had counselled cowardice, which was no more than might have been expected from a civilian. (As a working arrangement it was conceded that I had some kind of commission in the Space Navy, but no one knew, yet, the exact status).

I did not know of the general staff's decision to use the H-Bomb until later.

I picked up Sara from the Entourage Waiting Room, and we left. We were being driven by our respectful Space Cadet down an almost deserted street when the trumpet called up yonder.

With the first note he crimped the wheels sharply over to the curb, braked the car to a halt, and with a gasped, "I gotta report to the Parade Ground," he slid out of the car and started running down the street. Apparently his Pavian response to a bugle call was in good working order, and apparently it has not been contemplated in his conditioning that he might ever be so far away from the parade ground when the bugle called that driving an automobile might have got him there faster. Naturally, since if he were that far away he couldn't hear the bugle call, could he? So the one-to-one response of "Run when you hear the bugle" had been deemed sufficient.

All this was the merest flash in my mind, as Sara and I climbed out of the car, for the golden notes flooding us filled us with an ecstasy to drive out every other thought.

We stood there on the curbing and gazed upward into the heavens.

There were the projectiles, dimly red in the night sky, seeming to draw together now. But high above them, apparently so high they still caught the light from the sun below our horizon, a new set of ships had appeared. Each an iridescent globe. They flew in a wing formation; a vast wing. It was like a wing of shining pearls.

They came closer. They began to shade into an iridescent blue.

And like the star sapphire, even at this distance we could see the symbol on each of them—a shining white cross of radiant light.

"Oh, Ralph," Sara breathed. "How beautiful!"

"Come on," I gasped and pulled at her arm. "Get under cover. They're going to attack the projectiles!"

I knew, I don't know how.

STANDING in doorways, under awnings and canopies, leaning out of windows, the other people knew, too. We ran, as people run in a drenching rain, to take shelter under an archway which led into an arcade of shops. Yet, no more than there, joining some others, we turned and craned our heads to look upward again. The protection of the arch was of less value than the sight. We stepped back out into the clear where we might see the whole dome of the sky. All thought of personal safety was lost in the sheer, blinding wonder of the spectacle above. We were dimly conscious that the other people, too, were creeping out of hiding places, to stand in the open streets, rapt in awe.

The vast wing of iridescent globes, at first so high it was like a piece of jewelry set with pearls, sapphires, opals, was now close. They were swooping downward, but without spin, twist, or obvious force. Somehow this movement without thrust of force heightened the illusion of their serenity. The symbol of their crossed, white lines gleamed brighter now, telling us it was not an effect of the distant sun, but a glow which came from within them, a radiant purity of purpose.

Yet the red projectiles had not been thrown into panic and confusion by the sudden appearance. Now it became clear to us people in the streets below why the discs had hovered and waited over the city all these hours. Through some source of their own, they must have known that the radiant globes were on their way to attack them. Sharply, with its own effortless burst of speed, but this time sinister rather than serene. The Black Fleet, black in the day and dull ember red in the night, veered off in a long arc of flight; hurtled westward; formed into tight combat units of four or five ships each; faced around to meet the challenge.

We had first thought it was the flight of cowardice, now we realized it was the viciousness of the cornered rat.

Down in the streets below the people murmured their thoughts and hopes and fears to other people, man spoke to man, neighbor to neighbor, without first calibrating the number of pigment cells per square inch of skin or demanding status credentials. The ground swell of conviction grew that this was not the first time these two alien forces had joined in battle. Had Milton in his dreams of Heavenly Hosts and Satan's Minions been visited with some reality of this long ago and far away? We knew, everyone knew, this was one of a long series of such engagements.

There was no question of whose side we were on, who we hoped would win, must win.

There grew the conviction this was the decisive encounter. This was to be no hit and run skirmish, settling nothing. No, this was it.

Either The Black Fleet must be vanquished or it must be driven so far away that it would never return to threaten Earth's people again. Where were the scoffers now who doubted that the universe had been constructed solely for the benefit of Man, and that Man, as its Supreme Achievement, must not be harmed?

On came the star sapphire globes, huge now that they were near, leveling their dive enough to offset the enemy's shift to the west. It was obvious that the new path of descent would hurtle them headlong into the discs in a few seconds more.

Long tentacles of blood light flickered out from the projectiles, the darting tongues of snakes. In and out they flashed, so many they surrounded the discs, creating a deadly, protective screen of twisting, corrosive fire.

As if they could not stop, or had a courage beyond human comprehension, the vanguard shock unit of the globes smashed into the fire-tipped tentacles. And the impact flooded the streets below with a sound of molten steel being poured into icy water. There was a flare of intolerable blindness.

And when our eyes cleared and we could see again...

There was nothing left of the first wave of globes.

As if it possessed but one throat, one voice, from the city below there was one long groan of anguish.

HEROICALLY, the other globes did not hesitate.

Another wave plunged into the writhing tentacles. This time the blinding flash seemed less. Perhaps, expecting it, we slitted our eyes against its coming? This time the destruction of the new wave of globes seemed not instantaneous, nor, did they wink out completely. This time there were vapor clouds billowing white against the black heavens as the second shock unit more slowly disintegrated. It was destruction, but not so easy; perhaps no more than the force of an ordinary atomic bomb. The mushrooming clouds of vapor, boiling upward, seemed the same.

A third wave of globes came in. Ah, the courage, the guts! From the streets of the city there was the murmur of wonder, hope renewed.

The discs did not waver in their defensive formation. They seemed to draw a little closer together. A screen of dead black against the lighter sky flickered first, then joined ship to ship.

We groaned in despair.

Our despair was realized.

This time there was no sound of molten steel in icy water, no billowing clouds of vapor, no blinding flash of light. At first touch of the shining globes against the dead black blood screen, the globes were no more.

Yet not in vain. Now we saw one solitary globe still alive, coming from another direction, taking advantage of that instant when the Black Fleet had concentrated all it defensive screen against the wing of onrushing globes, somehow getting behind, inside the defensive screen.

To loose a violet white radiance.

And for a long, interminable, hopeful instant, the radiance persisted. We saw four of the black ships explode into poison foetid gobbets of rotten offal.

The other discs wavered, then the pack swarmed all over the gallant, lone globe. And still the hopeful instant endured the squirming nest of blood black tentacles.

And then hope died.

The radiant light faltered, flicked. The globe surface seemed eaten away like swimming spots of black on an aged bubble.

Then, like the bursting of the bubble, it, too, was no more.

WE clung together there in the street, Sara and I, drawing human comfort from the contact, staring upward; completely engrossed in the titanic battle—the incredible heroism of the globes—the incredible power and malignancy of the discs to withstand them. The ache of our shoulders and necks was as nothing in the throat pain of our apprehension.

It seemed not to occur to anyone, then, to wonder that the air about us was still fresh and clean, that we had felt no atmospheric shocks, that there were no falling objects of debris, that even the scabrous gobbets of offal from the exploded discs had somehow disappeared before reaching Earth.

High in the heavens, another wing of pearls appeared.

"This time they must win, they must!" Sara was moaning.

As with the previous wing, this one sank toward Earth and battle.

Then hesitated!

Wavered in indecision!

Then seemed to withdraw. A long, wailing groan from the city below seemed surely enough to reach up to them. How high can a prayer fly?

"No-o-o! Oh-no-o-o!" Sara was echoing the groans of despair all about, us. "They can't fail us now!"

"They won't!" I exclaimed in complete certainty. "You'll see!" And then I added something all out of context with how I felt, how we all felt. Something, which filled me with self-loathing, made me despise myself. "The script calls for it." I said.

And fortunately no one heard me. Not even Sara.

And I was right.

As the jeweled wing faltered, seemed about to break apart in confusion, the discs shot forward, lured out of their protective formation, blazed their blood red rays outward for the kill.

And a score of the globes, darting away in all directions, as if utterly demoralized; suddenly reversed direction at incredible speed, and converged upon the now scattered discs. From high above, wing after wing of globes swept in until the sky was filled, crowded with darting globes and discs, enjoined now in mortal conflict of individual duel.

As if some protecting screen of our own had rotted and burst now, all at once, our own atmosphere was sulphurous with choking gasses. We felt the blasts of heated air sweep down. Yet, after our first panic flight back to protecting overhangs, our first surprise that we still lived, not unendurable.

And then somehow, to increase our sense of participation, identification with the battle.

The dueling battle endured. How long? How long?

Time had ceased to exist. Body need had ceased to exist.

SOMETIME during the night (perhaps in early morning hours?) the arena of battle moved toward the west. Now it was centered no longer over the city. Now it was fading over the horizon.

Now it was gone.

"We're not to know how it comes out?" Sara murmured plaintively, querulously.

"We'll know," I said strongly. And this time caught my following, despicable remark before it left my throat. "This is the intermission."

I started to say, "Let's go out into the lobby to get some popcorn," but had sense enough to change it into something rational.

"However it comes out, Sara, you and I will have a hard day at the Pentagon tomorrow. We may get no sleep, but we should try to find something to eat. We have to keep going."

We were lucky that the thought occurred to us before it had to many others. We stood up, stretched our aching muscles, and with stiff, unwieldy legs we threaded our way through the dazed and huddled groups of people to the community kitchen. We hadn't expected to find any attendants on duty, but the cybernetic cooking machinery was apparently unresponsive to the battle going on over our heads. Nor had there been a complete breakdown in supplying the machines with the raw produce.

Coins in the beef stew slot produced the usual containers. We sat at tables in front of the kitchen television set.

A montage program was in progress to bring us up to date. Everywhere the battle was the same. Everywhere it had moved away over the horizon to the west. What we had seen here in Washington had been witnessed over every large city on Earth. No one commented on this strange coincidence.

For all her usual sharpness, Sara seemed not to have caught it either. I held my peace. I was a cynical so-and-so. It was not the first time I had found myself out of step with the prevailing mood. I had learned my lesson long ago. I knew something of mob reaction, I'd seen it. I knew how little it took to turn an over-wrought, tense collection of individuals into a ravening mob, all acting in one accord of insane fury, possessed by a super-entity created through interaction and feedback of emotions, given brief life of uncalculated power, taking possession of the individuals, turning them into body cells of the entity, playing out the tragic role before the individual mind could recoil in horror from its acts, shatter the group accord and destroy the entity—after the deed had been done.

I held my peace and kept quiet.

BUT I no longer believed. I no longer believed that anything we had seen was real. I didn't know what it was. I had no idea of any power, which could produce an illusion of instantaneous worldwide scope; nor, as say, the purpose of doing it. I was convinced only that it wasn't what it seemed, that it was an illusion. That it was some kind of universal brainwash.

I looked sharply at Sara. I looked at the handful of people who had also thought of food and strayed into this kitchen. All of them were following, straining to follow, the words of the television commentator. All of them completely hooked.

How had I escaped? Why was I immune to the bait? Was it because a long and heavy career of working with great numbers of people, handling them, manipulating them, causing them to re-spond in the manner I chose—and discouraged and sickened with them because they did respond, because they had too little critical judgement of manipulative patterns to prevent them from responding—had this given me an insight? Was it that? Or was it some basic flaw in me, which moved me ever so slightly out of phase with my own kind; never again to be as one with them?

How well I understood the contempt of the politician for his constituents, the advertising man for those who bought his product, the entertainment producer for those who became enrapt with his creation. And yet, were not these shaped and debased as much by those to whom they pandered, as were their masses shaped and debased by them? By striving to pander to the widest appeal, the lowest common denominator, did they succeed in anything beyond lowering and debasing even that?

I knew some of the writers and producers around Hollywood. I was not particularly critical of them for giving the public what it demanded. Anything for a buck had become the national way of life. But I had been horrified that although they maintained a superior attitude, and a condescension toward the low level of the public mind, their own taste and critical judgement became debased by their output until they, themselves, began to think it was good. They, themselves, became the victims of their own illusions.

Why was I immune? I could not even join with these!

We were breaking apart the dessert container, when a cacophony of voices from the street penetrated the open door and overwhelmed the voice of the television commentator.

"They're coming back! Ah-h-h! They're coming back."

OUTSIDE, on the street again, we saw it for ourselves. Yes, they were coming back.

In spite of the thoughts I had had, sitting there in the kitchen and watching the others while they watched the television, in spite of this I felt my pulses quicken, my heart began to pound, a choking gladness. There was something in the atmosphere to which my animal responses quickened even while my intellect held back—and the emotional responses began to erode, to wash over, to drown critical judgement.

Yes, they were coming back. And I lifted to them, eager to meet them. Everyone was on his feet now, with their eyes turned toward the west, straining toward the west.

But as the battle forces drew closer, the rising hope and excitement changed again to dread and despair. The globes were pitifully few now, so pitifully few. Still outnumbered. Still outpowered. Still having only one weapon superior—their incredible courage.

Now we could see the projectiles make their move, almost as if we could enter that evil, alien mind; we could see them make their decision that now it was time to move in and crush the radiant globes—utterly. So, like an angry den of snakes, squirming and writhing, they swarmed all over the globes, inundating them.

And still a few, a pitiful few, of the globes escaped somehow. Escaped, but not to flee. Escaped, but only to turn and reengage their enemy.

They began to win.

The faces of the people in the street were slack with awe. Their glistening eyes were sick with hope denied, hope still struggling to hope. To despair again and again, all through the night, and now, with the first breath of silver in the Eastern sky to see the tide turn. Dared they hope? This time, if despair swamped it once more, the very roots of hope would die.

Yet hope they must.

AND now I knew what I had not known before. Why the constituents voted in the politician. Why they bought the advertiser's product. Why they even supported Hollywood's shabby little travesty.

Better to have hope and faith that sometimes...maybe...

Than none.

Now I knew the meaning.

The deed proved the virtue. The virtue proved the deed.

If your heart is pure, your cause is just, your strength is great, and your purpose firm; you can overcome the obstacles in your path to reach your heart's desire.

This was the essence of all religion, all philosophy, all education, all science, all man's striving. If man did not believe this, then there was no meaning to anything. Without this belief, nothing mattered, man was nothing.

There was a hunger, a craving hunger in man to be reassured of it, to be told it again and again. He could not get enough of the telling. He became the willing, the eager victim of those who traded in the hunger, sickened in knowing he was being victimized, humbly supplicating to be victimized again, because maybe...this time...

Even the shoddy, shabby trivialities of Hollywood, the nasty little shyster tricks of writers and producers in stringing together meaningless story formula. Even these, for they, too, promised...

THERE, above us, it was being played out once more. Never had the forces of right and evil been so obviously enjoined. Never had evil been so near to triumph, nor good so valiant in near vanquishment. Never had heart and strength fought with such firm purpose in just cause.

Now the obstacles were being overcome.

For others, in other longitudes, the space suspended Earth turning in the sun's light as it does, and yet all this happening simultaneously, the battle must have been fought from dawn to dusk in the brightness of day, from morning until evening, from noon until midnight, from afternoon until the low ebb.

FOR us, there in Washington and along the Eastern seaboard of the United States, it seemed to have a special meaning.

For the turning point came with the first streaks of silver up the morning sky.

And confirmed for us that this time our faith and hope was justified as the sky grew in light.

All at once we knew that, this time, the battle would not reverse itself again. With so few of the globes remaining, and the hosts of evil discs which seemed to spawn still more to take the place of those destroyed, we did not know why or how the tide of battle turned.

But turned it had.

And with the first golden ray of the rising sun, the discs streaked away from the globes in cowardly fear. Their passage through the upper atmosphere came back to us in a scream of insane, craven terror.

And after them pursued the globes.

Now we could see them no more. Only here and there were bursts of flame brighter than the sun's light, gouts of red fire like opened arteries of blood. The sun bathed the city streets in its warmth. Now the people who had watched all through the night began to move sluggishly about, as if wakened from a dream. They looked at one another, as waking members of a family might, and for the moment the close affection of family replaced the endless, irritated, sibling bickering among them.

I looked at Sara. Her face was drawn with weariness, and I suppose she saw the same in mine. But I doubt she found the same contentment and fulfillment in my eyes as I read in hers.

There seemed nothing to say. The magnificence of what we had seen obviated all comment, all evaluation. It needed no interpretation of meaning. Not to most, whatever complex wonders and doubts I might feel.

This was not of Earth. That much was clear. No group of men, no nation could have staged this production.

They had come from the stars.

They had come, but not in the way I had imagined they might, someday. I had thought they would come, if they ever came, in reason and rationality, beyond selfishness, beyond passion, beyond falseness. They had come, instead, in fire and passion, in war and destruction, spewing forces at one another beyond comprehension.

And completely phony!

A staged production, specifically for our benefit. A magnificent production, beyond all the wildest hopes of our own showmen— and as phony as anything that ever came out of Hollywood, where they prefer the phony even when the real, the rational, the believable would do the better job.

Yet what kind of alien mind could so accurately assess the human response as to know it would respond favorably to the phony where it might reject the real? How long had they been studying us without our knowledge? How deeply had they dug into us? They had used the very basic drive, which had brought man up out of the slime to reach for the stars—faith in the triumph of virtue. To gain?

What? What did they plan to gain?

Or had we become so disillusioned in our ideals that we could contemplate no motive beyond self-gain?

There was nothing to say beyond the trivialities of routine.

"WELL, Sara, things will be popping today around the

Pentagon. And if I remember right, we are the authorities on extraterrestrial psychology."

"Supposed to be," she agreed with reservation. "Do you really understand all this? Well enough to tell the staff what it is all about."

"Not that well," I said. "Just well enough to say right now that we can expect visitors shortly. From the globes, not the discs. Not well enough to know what they want from us. But well enough to know that we'll give it to them, whatever they want. They've seen to that."

"Well naturally we would," she said reproachfully. "After what they've done for us. Who could hold out or bargain? What with? And who would want to?"

"Still," I said, "they'll be pounding on my door; I mean Earth-men, not Star-men. I don't expect ever to get within shouting distance of the Star-men. But the Earth-men are going to want me to brief them on how the Star-men's minds work."

"You think you can do it?" she asked doubtfully.

"Hell, no," I said frankly. "But, just the same, we ought to be getting to work. Which means digging up some kind of trans-portation."

We walked back toward the community kitchen, and as we passed we looked inside. A taxi driver, we could tell by his cap, was nesting a mug of coffee between his hands, warming them as he drank the liquid to warm himself. We went in and sat down at his table.

"We work at the Pentagon," I said to him. "We're trying to get to work. You willing to drive us?"

As if unwilling to take his eyes away from the visions of remem-brance, he merely stared.

"This is Dr. Kennedy," Sara explained. "He is an officer in the Space Navy Bureau of Extraterrestrial Psychology. He is needed at the Pentagon. You must drive us there."

That did the trick. He leaped to attention.

"Is your cab parked nearby?" I asked.

"About a quarter block up the street," he answered.

"Lead the way," I instructed.

By comparison with the still dazed people on the streets, he was as sharp as a tack. We climbed into his cab.

"You do know where the Pentagon is," I said, as he pulled away from the curb.

He looked reproachfully at me through the rear view mirror.

CHAPTER ELEVEN

THE PEOPLE on the streets were beginning to move about more actively now. There were lines forming at the doorways of community kitchens for morning coffee. Here and there, other cars than our own were beginning to move. The morning duty was replacing the night's dream.

PAWN of the BLACK FLEET

By MARK CLIFTON

Illustrated by FINLAY

I snapped on the taxi television set, and as it warmed to life, one of the World Broadcasting Company's commentators was giving a rundown of happenings around the world.

Everywhere the pattern had been played out in the same way. Everywhere, at the same instant the discs had fled and the globes pursued.

Yet there was a curious lack of something (enthusiasm, gladness, gratitude?) in the commentator's voice. At first I thought he was characteristically under playing it, just giving the facts, ma'am, and then I realized there was a deliberate reluctance to express a reaction—as if he hadn't been informed as yet on company policy; and knew from experience that he'd better not have any opinion until he had been told what it ought to be.

I was about to reach over and snap him off when a stir among the increasing crowds on the street distracted me. Over the cadenced tones of the commentator, I heard a hoarse scream from a man on the sidewalk. A hoarse ecstasy. And other voices took up the cry.

"They're coming back! The Globes!"

Without being told, the driver pulled over to the curb. On the screen I saw the face of the commentator beginning to fade and a globe beginning to appear. There was a flickering, a streaking of colors, as if the broadcast engineer were trying to maintain control of his sound and picture in spite of overpowering interference. Interference won. The sapphire blue globe with its star of radiant light steadied and glowed on the screen. I did not snap it off.

"I gotta see this," the taxi driver said. The dream had overwhelmed the duty once more. He threw open the door and slid out of his seat to stand on the curb.

We were about to follow him, Sara and I, when a new voice came through the television speaker—a voice resonant, calm, reassuring...

"*We come from the stars...*"

The voice was in English—American English.

"*We mean you no harm...*"

This was the second sentence. It was followed by another pause. Then came two short sentences, followed by some semblance of explanation. The streets outside were as still as vacuum, except for this voice which penetrated everywhere, transcending the laws of electronic sound.

WE come as friends. We will not hurt you.

"We return as ambassadors from our fleet which has gone in pursuit of our enemy—your enemy.

"We ask permission to land at your Capital City, Washington, District of Columbia, United States of America.

"We can only spare this one ship, with its crew of five, from the battle.

"We know you would prefer us to land at the United Nations, but there are compelling reasons why it must be Washington.

"We would give offense to none, by this, and hope you will grant our need.

"We will now withdraw to give you time for considering this petition.

"We will return in twenty-four hours, and wait the broadcasting of your permission, on any of your electronic channels.

"If you refuse, we will go away, without harming you.

"We hope you will not refuse. That you will permit us to land.

"We would like to meet you and greet you."

There was another pause, while the motionless natives thought this over. Then again came the careful, reassuring sentences:

"We mean you no harm. We come as friends."

The globe receded then.

There was dead silence in the streets for a moment after the voice ceased and the globe disappeared into the heavens.

Then a roar broke loose. There was no question of its welcome. The people were screaming in a frenzy of jubilation, embracing one another, pummeling one another.

I looked at Sara. There were tears in her eyes.

"They didn't demand anything," she said. "They could have. They could have landed without asking permission. What's to stop them? But they asked."

"Um-hum," I agreed. "And there's going to be holy hell to pay because they're landing here instead of at the United Nations. First mistake I've seen them make."

"They said they had their reasons," she reproved me.

"Um-hum," I said, "I suppose they have. They've played it too cagy all along to pull a blooper like that unless they had a reason."

Sara looked at me as if I were something white and crawling which had come out from under a rock.

How was I to know that while they were staging their big production over the major cities all over earth, this had taken only part of their attention, and that the remainder of it had been engaged in sifting and sampling through the minds and emotions of human spectators below. That unshielding these minds and emotions had been one of the reasons for the production. That they were looking for a particular reaction to the production.

How was I to know that my doubt and cynicism of its reality was one of the first to register? That my being out of phase with my own kind brought me closer into phase with them?

How was I to know that their reason for landing in Washington was because that's where I happened to be?

CHAPTER TWELVE

THE Starmen's diplomatic request for permission to land on the sovereign territory of the United States of America had come at 7:42 A.M.

At 8:00 A.M., the Home Office Policy Board of World Broadcasting Company (and affiliates) were assembled in their usual semi-circle of seats facing Harvey Strickland's empty desk in his penthouse office atop his New York W. B. C. skyscraper.

This time the boss did not keep them cooling their heels. He swept regally through the doorway in his purple dressing gown and took his throne seat before them.

They fervently put their all into a bright and cheerful organization-man's "Good morning, H. S." This few were permitted to H. S. him, a mark of his confidence in them. Most often he observed the important executive tradition and ignored their greetings, but this morning he gave them a cheerful nod as reward.

It revealed his mood and set the tone. It insured, in advance, that their independently thought out editorials, the factual news articles, the independent commentaries and feature articles, the colloquially worded amateur-writer sentiments of Constant Reader letters to the editor, all these would reflect, confirm by selected fact, buttress by independent column and commentator philosophies, and substantiate that the right thinking public were all in unanimous agreement with Harvey Strickland's policy.

Harvey Strickland was jubilant. For all the power they had displayed, the Starmen had, nonetheless, revealed themselves as weak and uncertain. He, himself, would have landed, then and there, while the Earthmen were dazed and spent, when they had had no time to organize resistance or policy, at any time and place he chose to land without asking, without explaining. The Starman had not done so, and were therefore—weak.

His confidence in his power and destiny all but overwhelmed him.

"They want something from us," he said in his opening sentence. "They want it bad enough to beg us for it. We've got something they want, and we've got it right here in America. No place else, now. Remember that. Right here. Along with deciding whether we will let them have it—and at what price, remember that, gentlemen, at what price ?—we've gotta fend off those thieving foreigners who will try to get in on it."

HE broke off to gaze in exasperation at the ceiling.

"Sometimes it's too much," he groaned. "It's hard enough to get those knuckleheads in Washington to do the right thing, but at the same time we've gotta keep the foreign nations in their places, too."

He squared his shoulders and became man enough to carry that extra burden.

"First question:" he resumed. "Shall we give them permission to land?"

Nobody answered. Naturally. They weren't expected to.

"Shall we give them permission to land?" he repeated. "The answer is—yes. They've said they would go away if we didn't. So far, we have to take them at their word. Within reason," he chuckled slyly. "Within reason." He stuck his tongue powerfully into one cheek. "We don't know just what they want, want bad enough to beg for it. We'll give 'em a chance to beg, before we make up our minds on letting 'em have it."

The policy board nodded in agreement with the wise decision.

"Cautious optimism, gentlemen. That will be our policy. We greet them as distinguished foreigners have to be greeted. Distinguished foreigners with their hand out. We don't notice that they've got their hand out; not right away. We think they're coming to see us because they like us. I guess all you fellows know that routine well enough.

"Now official Washington will want to make a big hoopla out of the visit. Maybe even more than usual. We'll go along with that. Just remember not to get carried away. The knuckleheads down there have the habit of getting carried away, like kids when their team wins the game. We've gotta keep a little rein on them, keep them from giving away the country. Welcome Stranger, but cagy, see? Any questions?"

He didn't expect any. But this time there was one. It came from the head of his legal department.

"I'm sure you've already thought out the legal implications involved in their preemption and use of our broadcasting facilities without license or permission, H. S.," the man said. "Our department will want to be briefed."

Strickland hadn't thought of that before, after all, it had been considerably less than an hour since the deed, and even a genius can't think of everything at once.

"Sure, sure, Bob," he answered genially. "But the same policy goes for your department. Let's don't file suit right off. Just hold back a little on that. We just might need that little item, at some point when we get down to negotiating. Start working on it, but hold back. Any more questions?"

AND still there was another. "What if they're not human?" asked one of the world renowned commentators who had made his reputation in crusading courageously for home, flag and mother. "What if they're—well, say, green spiders?"

A derisive titter greeted this absurdity, but the commentator, noted for his original thinking, stood his ground. He was relieved that the boss accepted the question seriously.

"It sounded like a human voice," Strickland said thoughtfully. "But they could have a machine of some kind. We've got machines, you know, that will turn a printed page into a spoken voice; so I guess they might be that far along, too. That don't mean they're human. Of course," and now he displayed one of those rare glimpses of how deep his learning really went, "Our best philosophers have all agreed that life on other worlds would have to develop the same kind of human body and human mind as we have, if it was ever to amount to anything. The philosophers we'll pay any attention to, anyhow, all say that.

"Still, we got to be grown up about this. We gotta be—big. They just might turn out to be—well, as you say, green spiders.

"So just barely touch on that. Hint that the public ought to be prepared, just in case. Not enough that anybody can claim we came right out and said they were green spiders, in case they aren't, but hint. They're distinguished visitors and all that. We got to be grown up enough, cosmopolitan enough, not to notice whatever's wrong with them.

"Now, any more questions?" This time he stood up and turned to leave the room.

There were no more questions.

WITHIN an hour, his private plane landed him at the Washington Airport. There was no company car there to pick him up. He made a mental note of that. It showed that already his Washington organization was going to pieces. Of course he hadn't let his New York staff know he was leaving, or his Washington staff know he was coming—he didn't have to account for his movements to the damn underlings—but they should have guessed he might come to Washington to see everything for himself, and had a car there just in case.

Time for that, later.

He picked up a cab at the airport.

"You got a reservation at the Hotel Brighton?" asked the driver.

Strickland didn't answer him, but this was a gabby one, and didn't seem fazed by the silence.

"You better have!" the driver rambled on, as he threaded his way through the outgoing traffic. "They've already started turning people away. All the hotels have started doing that. I swear I don't see how so many people got here so fast."

Strickland began to wonder, himself, where all the people could have come from. He couldn't remember ever having seen the streets so crowded; and after a night with no sleep for anybody, too. At the Connecticut Avenue traffic circle, traffic stalled again, and the driver turned around to face him.

"Say," he asked. "D'you think those Starmen will look like people?"

Strickland began to enjoy the driver. After all, a taxi driver represents the people of America, their hopes, their fears, their opinions, their intelligence.

"I don't have any idea," he answered with a chuckle.

A FRIEND of mine," the driver was saying, "Smart cookie runs a newsstand and is pretty sharp from being around all those books and magazines. He says maybe they'll be like big green spiders, with red eyes all up and down their legs. He showed me a picture on one of the magazine covers like that. Jeez!"

Strickland nodded and smiled.

"Jeez!" the driver repeated with more emphasis, now that his fare gave agreement. "I gotta wangle a place at the Mall tomorrow morning. That's where they're going to have the reception. How are them visitors gonna know where they ought to land?"

"We'll tell 'em on the radio. Remember, we have to give them permission to land?"

"Yeah, yeah sure," the driver remembered and nodded sagely. "I guess we'll send out a landing-beam for them to follow in. You think they might be smart enough to follow a landing beam down?"

"That's one I'm not going to worry about," Strickland said.

"Yeah, sure," the driver agreed instantly. "That's somebody else's problem." He thought for a moment. "Them fellows out at the Pentagon will probably check up on that one."

"Them fellows out at the Pentagon had better check up on quite a few things," Strickland answered ominously. He felt a stirring of something unfinished. Oh yes, there was some young punk out at the Pentagon he'd asked his secret service to check up on. They hadn't given him a report, yet. So now his secret service was falling down on the job. That had been yesterday, and no report yet. The battle of the globes and the discs was no excuse.

The traffic tangle unraveled, the cab jerked forward, and in a short while pulled up in front of the hotel.

"You gonna be there? At the Mall, I mean?" the driver shouted back over his shoulder.

"I'll be there," Strickland answered.

"Get yourself a good connection," the driver advised him with a sage nod. "Don't depend on your congressman or any of the common help like that. If you got a real good connection, you might make it."

"I'll make it," Strickland said confidently.

CHAPTER THIRTEEN

CIVIL Service being what it is, I thought it slightly miraculous that Shirley had already browbeat enough clerks into reporting for work to pass out forms of application for interview to the growing line of generals and admirals who wanted to be filled in on the latest estimates of extraterrestrial psychology.

Sara and I managed to get into the office not more than fifteen minutes after the final words of the Starmen, and already our day was beginning—the damndest day I ever went through. My something like five weeks in Washington had taught me a lot, but apparently not enough.

As the day progressed, in a fleeting few seconds here and there between conferences and conferences, telephone calls and telephone calls, I began to wonder how in hell the nation managed to keep going when apparently nobody was concerned with whether or not it got governed. Sitting there as I was, the answer-boy in the Bureau of Extraterrestrial Psychology, and therefore the final word on how we should conduct ourselves in relation to the Starmen, I got a pretty good cross section of what must have been going on all over Washington. A pretty good thermometer measuring the rising fever. I suppose I shouldn't have been surprised, I'd been around enough people not to be astonished at anything they might do, but I must have had an unsuspected residue of illusion left about the wisdom, level headedness, good sense and balanced judgement of those who govern us.

There had to be plans, of course, for a reception of the Starmen. I had no preferences in the matter, and the Mall sounded as likely a spot for the landing as anywhere else. There was plenty of space, which could be kept clear for the globe to set down, and plenty of space around the perimeter for the few dignitaries who would be permitted through the police lines.

Since the original planning took place there in the Pentagon, it was decided that a simple military welcome would be most impressive to the space visitors. Fighting men to fighting men. Just the Chief of Staff and the Joint Chiefs. With possibly a side dish of drill formation by the Space Cadets.

"And, gentlemen," I said firmly, "Representatives from the Bureau of Extraterrestrial Psychology. Dr. Kibbie, myself, my secretary, one or two others. After all, gentlemen," I answered their dubious frowns, "We are the first, the final, the only authority on the psychology of extraterrestrials. How will we be of further service to you if we don't get close enough to them to learn something of their psychology?"

They conceded that all right, it was logical enough that we should be there, but nobody else. Was that understood? It was all right with me.

APPARENTLY it was not all right with Congress. On a clear day the screams of outrage arising on the Hill might have been heard all the way to the Pentagon. Since there were telephones, it didn't need a clear day. Under the threat of new loyalty investigations, the military backed down, and conceded that picked committees, including the members of investigating committees, of course, could be represented.

The Secretary of State decreed that really the visit was more diplomatic than military. Hadn't the Starmen, themselves, already told us they had the status of ambassadors? What was military about that? Fighting men to fighting men, indeed! Since when did ambassadors fight? If anything, it might be the worst sort of diplomatic blunder to have military men on the scene at all; construed as a threat and all that. No, these were ambassadors from star government to Earth government, and protocol demanded it be handled as such.

This pulled the plug.

From 3100 Massachusetts Avenue came the cryptic question: Since when did the State Department of the United States represent Earth government? The Right Honorable British Ambassador, Knight Commander of the Bath, C. B. E., expected to be placed in line of reception at the Mall, and in a position commensurate with Empire Status.

Almost simultaneously, the white fronted, palatial Russian Embassy at 1225 Sixteenth Street announced that the true representatives of the toiling masses should be first in line to greet these sons of the Galaxy proletariat. The rather vague wording of this ukase gave the impression that an Inter-Universe Comintern had been responsible for Earth's rescue by the white globes, and only diplomatic sensitivity had kept them from wearing the hammer and sickle.

A rather feeble, and purely routine, request was filed by the Secretary of the United Nations, on the basis that since this was a world to world visit, didn't somebody think that the United Nations Organization ought to be the one to represent Earth? Just a suggestion, of course.

Nobody seemed to think so.

Norway, Saudi Arabia, Argentina were next to demand appropriate positions. The Ambassador from France was somewhat handicapped in that he didn't know who their Premier was today, and therefore didn't quite know whose name to use, but "Welcome in the name of France" had always been good, and he didn't intend to let the big powers use this occasion to brand France as a second rate power. Each of the two ambassadors from the Chinas spoke darkly of what would happen if the other were permitted to attend.

Official Washington, and all the nations, were conducting business as usual.

WITHIN the hour, every diplomatic mission in the Capital was hammering at the doors of the State Department, who, by their position, had lifted a considerable part of the load from my shoulders. The missions were being reinforced as fast as planes could empty the United Nations Building in New York and transfer the occupants to Washington.

In final desperation, since there was nothing else to do, appeals even filtered through to the President to make a decision on who should stand where in the reception line. Never one to make a decision anyway, this came at a most inappropriate time, for he hadn't yet decided the much more important question of which Image he wished to Project. For thirty-forty years the country, from election to election, had wavered between the affable but ineffectual Father Image, and the bright but annoying Kid-Brother Image. Should he radiate calm, fatherly indulgence; or should he be sharp and inquisitive?

If Official Washington was confused, Social Washington was more so.

There must be a dinner and formal reception in the evening after the arrival. From the distinguished alleys of Georgetown to the Hunt Club Set of Virginia and Maryland, the battle raged on who would sponsor it.

The social problems posed were stupendous. Who should be invited to the dinner? Should there be multiple dinners? Certainly not, this was no political election gimmick! For once and for all, status levels would be decided by who received invitations. It must be quite exclusive. But should they establish a secondary status level by inviting more people to the reception following the dinner? What about seating arrangements?

What would the Starmen wear? Would they come in smelly uniforms, or would they have black tie, or white tie? What dishes did they prefer?

What about this word going around that the visitors were really green spiders with red eyes running up and down their legs? Just on the chance, should the menu include—ugh—flies?

I suddenly created a new position for Sara. I switched such calls over to the Social Secretary of the Bureau of Extraterrestrial Psychology. She didn't thank me, but she did pick up on it with considerable more finesse than I had been able to muster.

Gently, firmly, she suggested on the matter of flies, for example, that they wait and see what the visitors really did look like. We didn't really have it on the best authority that they actually were spiders; but if they happened to be, weren't there just oodles and oodles of flies in the slums? And didn't Washington have some of the finest slums in the country? Let the flies wait.

ON THE matter of addressing the Starmen, for example. Your

Excellencies? No. How did we know they were excellent? Your Worthy Starshipsires? Awkward, and one simply mustn't be awkward. They finally had to let Sara arbitrate. She ruled a simple Sir should be adequate, until we knew more.

Should the women curtsy to the Spacemen? To spiders, my dear? Better wait on that momentous decision, too.

Now about dress? Wait a minute.

Sara looked over at me. For the moment I was between calls and conferences.

"They want to know how to dress," she said.

"Oh, dammit, Sara," I snapped. "For Chrissake! All right. Let the men wear tails. It'll be symbolic. Let the women dress the way savages dress everywhere—bedeck themselves in old dead parts of birds and animals, smear their faces with colored clay, mash flowers over themselves to conceal their natural stench. The same way they always dress. Now, for Chrissake!"

"Don't you think it should be formal, really formal?" Sara asked her caller sweetly.

The long, hellish day gradually drew to a close. The intervals between calls grew longer. I looked over at Sara during one of these intervals, and she was crying.

"S'matter, Sara?" I asked.

She looked up at me while she fished in her desk drawer for a tissue.

"Don't they remember last night at all? The courage? The beauty? The purity? You'd think…"

"I know," I said. "I'd like to go somewhere and hide, pretend I don't belong to the human race."

She wiped her eyes, and blew her nose.

"When I was a kid," I said, and looked back in memory to a long time ago, "I used to dream about the time when we would meet some other life intelligence face to face. I was pretty innocent, I guess. Because, in that imagining, I always saw man standing straight and proud—and I was so proud of him."

She lay her head down on her desk and sobbed uncontrollably.

CHAPTER FOURTEEN

THE President, or at least his phalanx of advisers, had made a protocol decision on who should stand where. It was 9:42 A.M. Radio contact with the globe, invisible somewhere out in space and unregistered on any of our tracking equipment, had agreed on 10:00 A.M. as a suitable landing time.

The President stood at the head of a flying wedge of dignitaries. He was flanked on either side by the key Senate and House leaders, appropriately spaced with an eye to the best camera angles. Behind the President, and blocked from view from any direction, stood the Vice President. Behind them were intermingled some five hundred Congressmen—not really intermingled, since seniority and party affiliation sorted them rigidly, although nobody but Congress would see the order of their standing. In a little group, by itself on one side of the Congress, stood the Cabinet. In a little group, on the opposing side, stood the Supreme Court. To the left stood the leftist country ambassadors, and to the right stood the rightist ambassadors—and if the uncommitted nations didn't know where to stand it served them right that they were left without any special place to stand.

Still farther off to the right, we representatives of the Pentagon stood. I seemed to be the only male in mufti in that contingent. Trouble was, they still hadn't officially given me a rank; and I wasn't sure I would be violating more sensitivities by assuming a uniform not officially mine, or appearing as a civilian. Apparently either way I was damned. Sara, loyally, stood proudly beside me.

"9:42," she said. "Eight minutes. But the globe is nowhere in sight."

"Insects are sluggish until the air warms up," I said, sotto voce. "Maybe 10:00 o'clock was too early."

She didn't bother to smile.

As far as we could see, in any direction, the Mall and all avenues funneling into it were packed with humanity. There was a ceaseless pushing, shoving, elbowing for better view. Each time a new VIP had arrived with police or military escort, those who lost their favored positions in making way fought to regain them. Most had got some sleep, since the night before had been all waking, but many had needed the fortification of alcohol to keep the little burner stoves of their souls alight. The crowd more nearly resembled the peak hour of an Irish clambake than a solemn reception of the first visitors to Earth from another world.

The landing area, itself, was a huge, slightly irregular rectangle, roped off with movable standards and chains. It stretched Eastward from near the steps of the Lincoln Memorial. The huge statue of Lincoln looked down on the scene, and the face seemed even sadder than usual at the sight.

Helmeted Space Cadets were drawn in parallel ranks just out side the roped area. They stood at Parade Rest, but the polished tubes of their ray guns were thrust outward toward the pressing crowd, silently warning the people not to come any closer unless they wanted to be paralyzed or disintegrated.

I looked at my wristwatch. Another minute had passed. The count down seemed to stretch outward to infinity.

"Maybe the Spacemen will understand," Sara said, as if to comfort me.

"I've been thinking," I murmured. "I'm pretty sure they understand more about us than I'm proud of."

PERHAPS it was my roving eye, I really don't hold with the superstition that we can sense when we are being stared at, but, just the same, I began to look around to see if I could spot that penetrating stare at me once more. I found it.

An enormously fat man was standing with a group of privileged newsmen over on the far side of the President's stance. There was no doubt about it, he was staring directly at me, as if trying to read down into the depths of my soul. It was my first glimpse of Harvey Strickland, although, then, I didn't know who he was. I was that ignorant of what really went on behind the scenes of democratic government.

"What time is it now?" Sara was asking.

"Six more minutes," I answered. The sweep hand of my watch assured me it really was running.

I looked away from Strickland—let him stare—and around the area again. The white marble steps of the Lincoln Memorial were lined with television cameras. More cameras peeked out from the observation windows atop the lofty Washington Monument. They were equipped with the latest lenses to present every detail of the landing in stark close-up, and no doubt the latest vibratory ears to record distant words spoken.

Beyond the official party, reporters with portable units threaded through the teeming crowd, picking up a babble of inane comment. A huckster was shouting, "Space helmets! Space helmets! Get yer soovineer space helments! Only fi' dollars while they last. Get 'em while they last, folks."

"It's three minutes, now," I said to Sara. "And still they're not in sight."

"They'll come," she said. "They're good. They wouldn't hurt us by promising to come, and then not do it."

"Yeah," I said drily. "They're the good ones. I'll bet they wear white hats."

"Sh-h," she whispered. "I understand how you feel, but other people mightn't."

"I don't know how I feel, myself," I said. "So how could you? I just have a terrible dread that this has all been one gigantic hoax, right from the beginning. And if it has been..."

The murmur from the crowd drowned out a sentence I didn't know how to finish. First a whisper, then a sudden roar, like fire bursting out of control.

"There it is! There it is!"

AUTOMOBILE horns began to blare across the city. Sirens swelled the volume of sound until ears were deafened. From somewhere out of sight, the Army cut loose with a 24-gun salute. The Marine Corps Band struck up its marching song. The Space Cadets began stamping their feet in their drill march.

I found the globe at last. It seemed to be coming directly out of the sun. Only by closing my eyes to slits could I follow its downward plunge.

And it was coming at unbelievable speed, a daredevil speed straight down at us—a foolhardy stunt speed; a teenage hotrodder manic speed; a showoff speed. Now that its angle was no longer against the sun, I could see its sapphire blue with the radiant star of light gleaming brighter than the sun's rays.

There was a stir in the crowd, that frozen moment before panic. Then, just at the instant when panic might indeed send us all crushing outward into the crowd crushing inward, the globe checked its hurtling descent, its flamboyant stupidity—and settled to the Mall as gently as a fallen leaf.

That impulse which had started up from our assembled guts as a scream of terror changed to a deep and satisfying sigh of awe and wonder.

As the globe settled, touched lightly against the pavement, it spiralled slowly until it presented the thin line rectangle of a closed exit hatch to face the Presidential Party. That group breathed a sigh of relief. Apparently these visitors, whatever they might be like, had enough sense to know who was important. Apparently it wouldn't start out with a faux pas, at least. Apparently the coming could be photographed and presented to the world as it actually happened, instead of being rerun and faked for public consumption at a later time.

I watched, hardly breathing.

A CURVED gangway materialized out of the side of the ship and dropped into position—gracefully, noiselessly.

The crowd, too, seemed to hold its breath. A long stillness of frozen motion. Only the cameramen seemed to make small movements as they huddled, crouched, aimed their lenses, and waited.

The exit hatch rolled back, and now we could see a blue light glowing softly from the interior of the space ship.

A soft rustle as the crowd seemed to lean forward.

Then the first Spaceman appeared.

He was human, tall, almost six-four, and built like a brick—and perfectly proportioned, beautifully muscled in all the right places. He was handsome with rugged masculinity. He was resplendent in platinum white uniform. Four circles of ebony braid decorated his tunic sleeves. On his left breast were row upon row of gleaming decorations. His shoulder insignia sparkled like diamonds in the morning sunlight. His white military cap, deep visored, was set slightly to one side of his head. On the visor was a radiant star in white gold, set in coruscating fire of a circle of diamonds.

The crowd remained hushed.

Over all the vast assembly there was no sound.

As the first Spaceman stepped down the gangplank, his stride a free and easy thing of strength, his eyes swept the crowd.

Was it imagination that they hesitated a moment on mine?

His eyes swept on around, and then his aquiline, perfectly chiseled features broke into a broad, toothy grin.

Signal for pandemonium. Caught breath, enmasse, was let forth in a gusty roar. Voices broke loose in a cackle of relief. Women began to weep, and scream with fandom adulation. Men hammered their hats into shapeless balls of felt. One small boy, obviously coached, threw a grubby handful of sticky, damp confetti; and in wild hysteria the people began to throw everything loose they had toward the landing field; watches, purses, tie-clips, hats. Most of it landed on the heads of others, slipped down and was trampled underfoot—but never mind.

I stood immobile, expressionless. I think I was the only one not shouting and screaming. Even the President was waving his top hat in the air and shouting what he remembered from a college sports yell.

The eyes of the grinning Spaceman came back to me, caught me standing immobile. His expression did not change, but his eyes seemed to question.

"Aren't I doing it right?" he seemed to ask.

But it was too fleeting for me to know. It had all happened during his first two steps down the gangplank.

His two steps ahead, and then, behind him, from the hatch, stepped two more Spacemen, and then two more. They were all dressed the same, except the four had only three ebony circles on their sleeves, some fewer decorations across their breasts, and only the star of white gold, without the circle of diamonds, upon their visors.

All were handsome, strong, virile, proud, beautiful.

There would be no need for feeding in the scullery: No need for Junior League or Junior Chamber of Commerce to go catching flies.

They came all the way down the gangplank in formation. The first Spaceman paused at the bottom, a little shyly, proudly but a little embarrassed.

But then, instead of stepping forward to the President, he made a sharp left turn, and all five of them marched over and came to a halt directly in front of me!

"Take me to your leader!" he said.

I looked at him. And to this day I don't know whether or not my lip lifted in a sneer. I looked at him, and then I realized that about two billion people were watching this—this charade, this farce. Certainly the eyes of everybody there were staring at us.

I took a deep breath.

"Come with me," I said. "I will take you to our leader."

I stepped up beside him. The four Starship crewmen fell in behind us. As one man, the General Staff from the Pentagon fell in behind them. We marched, with nobody out of step, to where the President was still standing. I halted in front of him.

"This is our leader," I said to the Starman. "Mr. President," I said, "May I present the men who have come from the stars."

At a prod from the House and Senate Leaders, the President took a step forward, doffed his top hat, and smiled his fatuous, vote getting smile.

"Men from the Stars," he rolled sonorously, "Earth welcomes you. Earth thanks you for defeating our enemy."

It wasn't too bad. Some White House speech writer had had enough sense to keep it simple.

The Spacemen listened, their heads bowed modestly, their shoulders square and erect. The First Spaceman took one pace forward, cleared his throat—and blushed!

The crowd was completely silent again.

"Shucks, Mr. President," he said in a West Texas drawl, "It wasn't nothin', really. Wasn't nothin' any red blooded boy in the Right Thinkin' Universe wouldn't have done for his friends!"

He broke into his exuberant grin again; that charming, careless, boyish, handsome, irrepressible, spontaneous grin which can only be achieved after hours upon hours of practice before a mirror.

"We was just lucky, I guess!"

CHAPTER FIFTEEN

THERE was something wrong with my consistency.

As soon as I grew certain, openly and honestly to myself, that it was all a gigantic hoax, I grew equally certain that it wasn't. Admittedly there was no Earth power, no mentality, no equipment, no facilities and no foolhardiness so great as to produce this hoax. That they had come from the stars I could not doubt. That they had deliberately hoaxed us I could not doubt. That they must have some alien motive for doing this I could not doubt.

And the more normal these slaphappy flyboys appeared to be, the wilder the acclaim and adulation of official and social Washington, and the world, the more I doubted them.

They were not, surely they could not be what they seemed. Then what were they? Why and how had they so completely adopted Hollywood's entirely spurious idea of what a hero should be? To conceal what?

To look through the eyes of what might logically be assumed the surveillance of an alien life intelligence, I might not be proud of Man (he gave me little cause); but Man was, nonetheless, my own. For better or for worse, I was on his side.

I longed to talk to someone about it, but as the day progressed I found no kinship doubt in any other eyes. I was one attending a suburban social who must tailor his tastes and opinions to public relations lest he give offense by seeming a minority.

Not even Sara was with me, not this time. There had been no doubt in her eyes, the last time I'd seen her before the crowd separated us at the Mall. Her eyes were star sapphires.

Unpracticed as I was in Washington's diplomatic courtesies, I found myself quickly shuffled, shouldered and edged away from the favored position the Starmen had given me at the Mall. Yet, to my astonishment, I found myself in the third car behind them in the parade on its way to the Blair House across from the White House. I learned only later that it was Shirley, who did know Washington, working behind the scenes, who not only saw to it that I got a seat in that car but who laid down the law to every host and hostess in Washington that one Doctor Ralph Kennedy must be hurriedly added to their exclusive lists. Only later did I learn that the servants and office staff members are the real social and political arbiters of Washington—everybody else is too green and inexperienced to know.

Both official and social Washington, after some cautious inquiry of their own servants, accepted Shirley's judgement. Word was passed around (and my status grew in the telling) that I was the world's foremost authority on extraterrestrial psychology...Adviser to the Pentagon...you noticed, didn't you, that the Spacemen picked him out to introduce them to the President, and they're certainly All Right...therefore he must be, too...

It seemed not to occur to anyone (else) to wonder how the Spacemen had known all this about me immediately upon landing—me standing there among all that resplendent brass and braid without so much as a good conduct medal.

IT WAS while driving from one welcoming function to another in the late afternoon of the first day that I made first mental contact with them. Unhappily, it was my last for quite some time. This time, through Shirley's influence, I had been given the seat beside the secret service man who was driving their open car through the crowded streets. We were driving through a wild demonstration of celebrity worship. Bex, Dex, Jex, Kex and Lex, seated in the rear of the car were busy grinning handsomely, smirking and occasionally saluting the crowd.

"You're setting us back a hundred years," I grumbled sourly, while I tried to look both brilliant and happy for the cameras, myself. "Here we've been telling our young people that the real hero of tomorrow is a Thinking Man; that to meet the challenge of the future they've got to develop their Intellect beyond studying out how to heat before they eat, how to obey road signs, how to distinguish between rest rooms. How far do you think we're going to get now, after the example you've set?" It was subvocal grumbling; no point in revealing myself to the secret service as a subversive.

We were still bowing and smiling to the crowds lining the street, but I forgot myself long enough to swallow hard on a doubletake at their answer. They did not speak it, but it was clear and sharp.

"The prevailing art forms of a culture invariably give the common denominator of its direction. In yours we find no such cultural ideal as you express."

It was the first thought they'd uttered which couldn't have been lifted bodily from the script of Git Along Doggie, or Riff Swift, Space Detective.

And it was impersonal, emotionless—as remote from approval or rebuke as a spiral galaxy.

There went my consistency again. Oddly, somehow; it made me feel better. At least they weren't really what they seemed— cowboys taken from some distant world's Western Plains, dressed up in fancy uniforms and taught to press some buttons. There was intellect behind those false fronts.

I felt a twinge of fear. So far they had taken utmost care not to harm any human life—but only so far.

They gave me no more contact. They were much too busy playing up to the crowds lining the streets. And why? Why were they working so hard to be popular? Why were they giving us such a liberal helping of what we obviously had hoped to find in them? Or were they sampling each mind as we passed? With the same ease in sampling mine? And finding? For what were they searching?

Too bad our scientists would all be back at the Mall, attempting to measure, guess the weight and composition of an entranceless, seamless globe. And I still wonder if their instruments told them there wasn't anything there—or if the instruments, too, were subject to illusion.

And I wonder, too, if the police department wasn't secretly relieved when the ship, in mid-afternoon, suddenly disappeared; releasing the cordons of police so they could go back to their normal occupation of attempting to entice ordinary people into committing crimes so they could entrap them more conveniently.

Now it was 3:00 o'clock in the morning. At the dinners and receptions the human males had worn their symbolic tails, the females had shown off the old dead scraps skinned from slaughtered rodents to display the hunting prowess of their males in the widows and orphans fleecing marts or under the graft table. The social events symbolizing the progress of a flowering civilization were over for the night. Even the stench of perfumes, so fragrant in the bottle and jar, so foetid as they oxidize and mix with sweat and decaying scales of skin, was being carried away on the cool night breeze.

The Star Heroes lounged around in one of the more intimate reception rooms of Blair House, theirs for their stay, while they relaxed before going to bed. Their long legs were thrown up over the arms of chairs, their cigarette ashes dropped carelessly upon priceless rugs, their corrosive nightcaps etched rings upon rare tabletops.

They seemed not to know about spy ray units, microphones and cameras concealed behind mouldings, under chairs, in electrical outlets, through minute openings punched through eye pupils of masterpiece paintings on the wall, through false mirrors placed strategically to cover every square foot of Blair House.

They seemed unaware that a couple billion people would be treated to their every private move and word.

The secret services, the super secret services, the spies who spy upon the spies, wherever a human body could be squeezed into false wall passages, locked closets, basements, attics and houses next door, all these watched, recorded and photographed for later analysis. They had begun with narrowed, suspicious eyes, they had savored each remark for hidden, subversive meanings, and gradually they, too, became convinced that these astronauts were, indeed, what they claimed to be—pure and simple representatives from the Right Thinking Universe.

I did my own share of listening, viewing, analyzing and wondering, and found I really didn't have the Peeping Tom temperament required for this work. My status as the world's foremost authority on extraterrestrial psychology gave me access to the various observing units, but after sampling the behavior of the Starmen, the cloud of avidity radiating from the observers drove me outside, onto the lawn, to clear my lungs with the night's cool breeze.

But not an empty lawn or street. Even at this hour of predawn, and after nights of sleeplessness, still there were crowds of people standing outside of Blair House stolidly watching, staring at lighted rectangles of windows blanked by closed blinds or even blanker walls.

I WALKED among the silent, staring people, and was on the point of deciding to find some transportation to my hotel when the dark figures of the crowd began to stir, and a low murmur arose from them. I turned and looked at the spot, which seemed to have drawn all their eyes.

It was one of the upper balconies, which let through french doors into a bedroom. It began with a glow, a vague nimbus of pearly light.

The throaty murmur around me was one of awe.

A form began to take shape within the brightening nimbus of light. At first it was ghostly, symbolizing immateriality. It began to clear, take shape. Now it was a human form. The arms came up and out. The white robe draped the figure and flowed from the extended arms. A face emerged from the nimbus of the head, a Flemish face, with hair long, and blonde, and draped in ringlets about the shoulders. The robe glistened now as finest nylon. A halo began to glow about the head.

Then it was gone.

The balcony was dark and blank.

The crowd had buckled at the knees. Some were lying prone upon the ground. I looked back up at the balcony angrily.

"Now what are you practical jokers up to?" I asked bitterly.

CHAPTER SIXTEEN

THE Miracle at Blair House, as it came to be called, gave Harvey Strickland the assurance he needed.

He sat, the next morning, in his purple robe at his desk in the suite of offices reserved for him at the Washington Evening Bulletin, and weighed the discrepancies in the vision against their purpose.

Nylon robe, indeed! His first response to this item in the reporters' stories had been fury at the sloppy thinking, and some of his reporters came closer than they ever knew to excommunication from the fourth estate. But then he grew curious at the unanimous opinion that the robe was nylon. Odd.

Odd, also, that a halo was universally reported. Painters didn't invent the halo for several centuries after the time of Christ. And it was some centuries still more before the anti-Semitic Nordic painters changed the physical appearance to one they liked better. Just as the approved image which came to be accepted had nothing whatever in common with the probably dark and swarthy little Asiatic Jew, so did Christianity evolve into something which had nothing whatever in common with that servile little Jew's teachings.

So what motive in presenting this wholly inaccurate vision? The damn Communists had said religion was the opiate of the people. As usual, they were so twisted in their thinking they had even misinterpreted this. Christianity was the most powerful weapon rulers had ever found for keeping the people meek, docile, humble, subservient, asking nothing, expecting nothing, fearing even that if they asked for their rights here on Earth, they might be denied them in Heaven. This was the reason the ancient rulers had shrewdly adopted it as a state policy; this was the reason the modern industrialist enforced it upon his employees, and saw to it that the ministers in his factory towns kept the workers humble, docile and afraid.

Suddenly he felt flooded with revelation. The Miracle at Blair House had been their sign to him. "We approve the method of scaring the sheep into submission," they were saying to him. "We see that there is altogether too much independent thinking going on, and it's time the people were brought back into line."

He pushed his huge bulk to his feet and began to pace the space between the desk and the doorway, while he thought out the implications behind the act. From their behavior these five had seemed no more than stupid flyboys, the kind of happy-go-lucky show-off's we might send out after we had taught them to press the right buttons. Maybe they were, maybe they weren't. Maybe there was more to them than met the eye, or maybe this was just another button they had been ordered to push, part of a long range pattern.

It didn't really matter which. Whether they'd thought it up, or it had been thought up for them, the intended result was clear.

Here lately there'd been a rash of independent little literary magazines, operating on a shoestring, with appeal to only a few intellectual-types. He'd paid them no attention. Those things usually died out after two or three issues and the backers saw that they hadn't changed the destiny of mankind with a couple of editorials. But the rash of them was symptom of increase in independent thinking. Worse, there were mutterings among the scientists that came close to mutiny. The damn scientists were getting too big for their britches. They were forgetting they were just hired mechanics, and were trying to tell the bosses how the shop ought to be run.

HE whirled around and slapped his hand down hard.

That was the deal!

Lest this give anybody ideas about science being more important than sheeplike docility, this arrival of men from the stars, the people were to be reminded of the pasture fences and who drives them with the dogs and whip.

Well, they didn't have to hit Harvey Strickland over the head. Now that they had shown him that either they, or the power behind them, knew the score; he'd play their game. Sooner or later, there'd be a showdown of hands across the table—or under it.

HE wheezed his high, gasping laughter, went around the desk, sat back down in the triple strength chair, and began punching buttons to summon his editorial staff. He grabbed up his phone, called his New York suite, and ordered Miller to come on the next plane.

He hadn't wanted Miller with him while he was uncertain of his course. It wouldn't do for Miller to know he could be uncertain. But now that he knew, Miller must be here to see. He would have considered it complete nonsense if any psychologist had told him Miller, to him, was symbolic of humanity; and that the same jealousy and hatred which had driven him to destroy Miller pressured his drive to humble the contemptible human race.

That its determined, eternal, beautiful effort to lift its head in pride, in spite of all his efforts and those down through the ages like him to keep it servile and cowardly, was embodied in Miller. Even if he had contemplated the idea, he would have rejected it, for obviously Miller had been completely broken, by him, long ago.

He would not have admitted, nor known, either of the human race, nor of Miller, that the spark of man's desire to lift himself up out of the muck, to throw back his head and gaze in ecstasy up to the stars, is never quenched.

More immediately, it did not occur to him that his secretary, so self effacing as to be often forgotten, as a good organization man should, had, ignored, stood by his shoulder once too often and watched him work the secret combination to his file room of dossiers.

That Miller had used his absence from New York, and the excitement of the rest of the New York personnel in its absorption with the doings of the Starmen, to spend long hours in that secret room.

That Miller had finally found his own dossier, and had read its every word with increasingly comprehending eyes.

That the dormant spark of pride in Miller had been given the fuel to flame into a raging fire.

CHAPTER SEVENTEEN

IT WAS Shirley again, with her manipulations behind the scenes, who filled my flowing days with woe.

Who had a better right to act as intermediary between the Starmen and the deputations and committees of Earthmen than Dr. Ralph Kennedy, the world's foremost authority on extraterrestrial psychology? True, the State Department, Commerce Department and Civil Space authority voiced loud protests, but Shirley solved all this by the simple, and thoroughly familiar to Washington, means of "transmitting orders from above"—without revealing who gave those orders up above. She simply told the guards around Blair House to admit no one but me.

Not even Harvey Strickland would be permitted to see the Starmen without securing my approval!

Trouble was, since I'd had no further contact with the Starmen, myself, I was hardly in position to start filling their calendar with dates from all the pressing deputations, committees, and individuals.

I found myself curiously reluctant to step out into the spotlight, for now the entire world sat staring at its television set which showed the entrance of Blair House and the milling crowds outside the cordon of guards.

So, the Space Cadets could escort me, and make a path through the crowds. So, the guards, upon proper identification, would allow me through the lines. So there I would be, walking up the steps, alone. Watched by two billion people. So I would knock on the door. So I would say, "Please Mr. Starmen, may I come in?"

What if they said, "No!"?

Damn you Shirley—you and your empire building.

I DELAYED putting it to a test as long as I could. My excuse was that I must sample the reactions of the press and television to the Miracle at Blair House.

The Strickland organization had gone all out. "Down on your knees, you stupid slaves," was the gist. "Grovel your silly faces in the dust. Lo! we have been given the sign."

The more I read the angrier I grew. Not only at Strickland, his motives were becoming pretty clear to me. Not just at the fanatics who were all too willing to jump on the bandwagon to increase their importance and their compulsion to destroy all who didn't acknowledge their ascendancy. But at the Starmen, themselves. What were they trying to do to us?

My anger supplied the necessary adrenalin to get me on my feet and going.

I was admitted through the lines and into Blair House by the Captain of the Guards.

I did not knock on the door, shuffle my feet, pull my forelock, make a steeple out of my hands and pray for admittance. I simply pushed open the door and walked inside. I had considered that they might throw me out bodily, feet flying over head down the steps, with two billion people watching my disgrace, but by now I didn't care.

Instead, I was received with that exasperating, "Shucks, Doctor Kennedy, we're just plain folks. You shouldn't ought to go to all this trouble, a busy man like you, just to see if we're makin' out all right."

They were scattered around the breakfast room, in dressing gowns. They were having morning coffee—black; served by the regular servants assigned to Blair House. Their faces were designed to reflect the morning after the night before.

My disgust with them increased, but I was stopped in my impulse to say what I thought by the knowledge of the spy rays, microphones and cameras.

"Funny thing about them gadgets," one of the Spacemen drawled, as a dark man in a white coat, who possessed far more dignity than I, seated me and gave me coffee. "Sometime during the night them gadgets all went out of commission. Them noises you hear behind the walls, I reckon they'r not rats—just electronic engineers tryin' to figger' out what went wrong."

That much was a relief. But the joker's stupid country boy accent and attitude wasn't. I'd caught that highly revealing flash about "cultural art forms" the day before, and they must have known I'd caught it. So they must also know that I wasn't taken in by their false faces.

So now why the masquerade? With me?

I didn't know what their game was. I knew only that so long as they maintained this farce, I wouldn't find out. I'm afraid I boiled over, as soon as the servants had left the room.

"YOU come in lies and deceit," I said, and was surprised to find I was speaking in cold, measured words instead of hot stammering. "I shouldn't be surprised to learn that you are also self-righteous, knowing what is good for us. And knowing that, capable of any atrocity upon us."

There was a blur of faces and forms. For an instant, there was no one in the room with me. Only a vortice of faint, violet light. Then the room was populated again. The boys were still lounging around with coffee cups in their hands. But their faces were not the stupid duh faces of Earth heroes. There was the faint glow of a nimbus around them.

It shook me. What kind of fool was I? To stir up what? All right! The worst they could do was blast me out of existence for blasphemy. And that might be preferable to living in the kind of world their behavior was going to create. Their faces were symbols of curiosity now, a wordless invitation for me to go on.

"The most despicable of all human traits, the most cruel and mean, is self-righteousness, the belief that there is some special virtue in ourselves which enables us to decide what is best for others. It provides excuse for anything we may want to do in the destruction of others. We know it well. We should. We've had plenty of experience with it. We know it in all its stages of progression. We know it is a contagion and an addiction. We know it to be worse than any narcotic habit, for it can only feed upon forbidding and condemning others in ever increasing doses; to increase its own self approval.

"You come to us in lies and deceit. You probably have even rationalized already that such lies and deceit are for our own good— the first stage of addiction to self-righteousness. You are, even now, probably trying to decide what is best for us. Your behavior seems to indicate you already think you know what is good for us. When will you go into the next stage of self-righteousness and start punishing us for not behaving the way you think we should?"

Again the blur, again the violet glow of whirlpool, again the curious faces around me. There was no country-boy drawl when one of them spoke.

"WHEN one of your biologists wishes to study a life form," he said in emotionless tones, "He first tries to measure all the elements in its environment. But this study does not reveal to him the tolerances of variation in that life form, nor does it reveal the potentials he suspects may be hidden within it. He enters the medium in which the culture exists, by, let us say, increasing the tempertaure, changing the chemical compound slightly, altering the environment to determine the potentials of reaction in the life form. He probably hasn't the slightest concern, at this point, for what is "good" for the life form, or "bad" for it. He simply wants to know what it is, how it behaves, how it might behave."

"And," I interrupted, this time a little hotly, "If he finds out we don't like it, we set about finding a way to destroy it."

They hit me then.

Oh not with a brawny hero's sadistic fists. They did not gun me down with impunity and praise because they were on the right side.

They hit me with a vision.

I saw the universe as I had never before conceived it. For an instant I knew the vastness of infinity, the trillions and quadrillions of whirling dead worlds, a vastness of emptiness so overwhelming that the mind cannot grasp the whole of it—and lifeless.

Only here and there, in such pitifully small quantities as to be only a trace element was there life in any form—and, of that, an even tinier amount evolved to self-awareness.

And then I saw Earth; with its surface teeming, crawling, squirming with multitudes and myriads of life forms; each in life/death struggle with all the rest for survival and room to grow. No wonder, to us, life was cheap. No wonder, to us, the way to win was destruction of our opposition. Our values were formed on a world where there was too much life for the space it could occupy.

Their values were formed by a universe almost totally devoid of life—where every scrap of it was so precious that its right to survive must transcend all else, the right to be must transcend the difference in being.

They did not know which was the Right form of life, and which the Wrong form. Such concepts had no meaning. They did not know which should become ascendant and which should be suppressed; for they did not know what the future destiny of life, any kind of life, was to be. They did not know it of us, they did not know it of themselves. They did not know of any right to harm us; or we, coming out to the stars, to harm them.

They did not know.

I did not know how or when I left them there in the breakfast room—again appearing to be duh loafers sprawled around sipping morning coffee.

THEY tell me that while I was there, for something like an hour, the crowds had massed in increasing numbers, to press tighter and tighter against the cordon of guards. They tell me that when I came out of the door, the crowd, which had been growing noisier, hushed. They tell me I walked as one in a trance. They tell me that even Strickland, purple faced near apoplexy in his argument with the guards, demanding admittance, fell silent, and clamped his lips in a thin line. They tell me that as I walked through the line, my eyes were fixed on something out of this world, and that the crowd, somehow, pushed back to open a path for me—wide enough that none touched me.

They tell me that, on the outskirts of the crowd, I stepped into the first limousine I reached—which wasn't mine—and that the chaffeur, without a word, closed the door and drove me straight to the Pentagon.

I came to, sitting at my desk, with Sara telling me that the deputations of politicians, business men, and even some scientists were still waiting for me to tell them when they were scheduled to interview the Starmen.

I shook my head, as if coming out of a sleep.

"I don't know," I said vaguely. "I didn't think to arrange anything."

"But, boss," she wailed. "You have no idea what we've been going through trying to stall off those people! It's been a deluge. Everybody demanding..."

"To hell with all of them!" I said.

MEANWHILE, back at the office, things had not stood still.

I had no more than introduced the Starmen to the President than Central Personnel suddenly discovered that somehow it had made the mistake of cutting my employee requisitions in half and that in view of my obvious change in status the credit they might receive for all that money they were saving the taxpayers might measure somewhat less than the blame for not giving me the help I asked. They hurriedly rectified this by sending more than a thousand new employees to us, in one day's time—each carrying a Back-Order reference to a given requisition.

Shirley was fit to be tied. But she arose to the occasion by appealing to Dr. Kibbie for assistance in finding still more space to hold them and orienting them to their new jobs. Apparently he was willing and eager to help, and to offer the help of all his other departments as well. We were making use of that two billion very nicely, and he had received word from a Congressional Committee that even though Congress was not officially in session all members were in town, and if we needed any more spending money they could get some of the boys together within an hour. Dr. Kibbie did not refuse. Shirley's request for him to take on some of the burdens and actually do some work around here, came as a boon to him.

Mine was the department where the spotlight was shining. He was only too glad for the opportunity to move back into the spotlight, after he had flubbed earlier chances so miserably. If it seemed that I had started out working for him and now he was working for me—well, that's Washington.

Shirley had done a couple other things to pull the reins of control tightly into our hands. Telephone switchboards were removed from Blair House and all calls were routed through our office, or rather, stopped at our office. All mail and telegrams were routed to our office. She closed off every approach to the Starmen except through us—through me.

Dr. Gerald Gaffey, the second member of my original staff of three, was not far behind her. He, too, in his own field, had become the man of the hour; and arose to its challenge. With a singular lack of self doubt and conflict, which usually keeps the intellectual impotent to accomplish anything, he drafted every available scientist to assist him in calculating the probable civilization of these Starmen to pad out the bales of news releases demanded of us; for page after page and hour after hour of print and discussion must be filled. There was no news of any other kind worth printing or talking about.

THE scientists were delighted. As rapidly as they could, they turned off their Bunsen burners cooled their retorts, balanced their equations, set aside their drawings, and flocked to his aid. When he matched them credential for credential, hauteur for hauteur, they fell to work with a sigh of deep satisfaction. Accustomed as they were to being low man on the totem pole, bottom of the status barrel, victims of every vagrant breeze that blew in cultural whims; they had grown practice in seizing every fleeting opportunity to add a little more to mankind's knowledge of the world and universe about him before a change in whim cut them off at the pockets, or a new program of anti-science in the culture quietly eliminated them.

A skilled archeologist, finding the fragment at the site dig, can deduce an entire culture from a single shard. To do this, they must have known that. To know that could only happen after they had progressed through these and these stages of cultural growth. Buried at this level, in this climatic condition, required this much passage of time. Or, finding this shard at this site, instead of half way around the world where it should have been found, presupposed an intercontinental trade among these earlier people, which, in turn, measured the level of civilization they had attained. All from a piece of shard—and astonishingly accurate in estimate, when later discoveries come to light. (Or, are later discoveries rearranged to confirm the first?)

Here they had no isolated shard. They had had days of watching, first the discs, then the globes, the battle with its incredible denials of the laws of inertia, the globe which had come to rest briefly at the Mall before it suddenly disappeared, the shape and clothing of the occupants—the speech of the occupants which they must have learned from a Western movie television wave trapped by their instruments, the correct (well, insofar as West Texas speech can be considered correct) semantic meanings to, the words they had uttered. Here was such an abundance of observation and evidence that education was mere child's play—at least deduction at the level understandable to the people.

Their scientific deductions even brought them dangerously close to the forbidden areas of the humanities. For they deduced two massive galaxial civilizations strung out among the stars and galaxies of stars, at war, one Evil, one Good.

The discs were Evil, because they had threatened us. The Globes were Good, because they had saved us. The scientists fell into the humanities routine of morals and ethics without even knowing they had done it.

They did not go on to spell out that mankind's morals and ethics are based solely in expediency and have no other source of origin; that which favors his survival is Good; that which threatens his survival is Evil. The universe was created around man, for his benefit and no other purpose. It surrounds him, he is at its center, and all things in it relate to him in terms of Good, or Evil. In the humanics man is still in the Ptolemic age and has not yet reached, or come close, to that level of rational thinking where a humanic Copernicus can emerge.

And therefore the scientists bought themselves a few more days of toleration from the humanists, by, once again, not challenging the arbiters of right and wrong.

THESE bales of news handouts kept reporters and commentators off our necks for the moment. But the insistence of other deputations, each with its own expedient fish to fry, was growing in volume and number.

Oddly, there were no church deputations. Perhaps the churchmen prefer their miracles be kept long ago and far away. Perhaps that bogus miracle at Blair House filled them with dread that the Judgement Day was at hand—a Judgement Day few of them really believed would ever come, when they would be called to account for what they had done with that stewardship handed to them so long ago. At least, so went the comment around the department when the absence of such deputations was realized.

One other little development of a minor nature had also been making progress. With incredible speed, work and skill, which can only come through complete dedication and psychotic drive, N-462 had now completed his proof that I was not the real Dr. Ralph Kennedy (who was still teaching a vague class at a vaguer college somewhere in the mid-west, and never knowing how much he was missing just because some clerk in Space Navy got the files mixed up), but only a Mr. Ralph Kennedy, an impostor.

Following the accustomed police pattern he calculated the various avenues of advantage to himself, brought the proof of my imposture to me first—and held out his hand.

"Hell!" I exclaimed after I'd looked it over. "I'm not going to pay hush on a half cooked job like this. If you'd used more sense and less venom you'd have checked Space Navy, Personnel Department, Section of Files beginning with the letter K. There you'd have found a recording of my telephone call, which I made when I first got their letter telling me they'd court martial me if I didn't show up in forty-eight hours. You'd have found I told them and told them that I was the wrong man.

"If you'd interviewed the people I saw, in person, after I got here, and used the proper thumb screws and rubber hoses in the approved police manner, they'd have finally admitted that I told them again and again I was the wrong man.

"They're the ones who made the mistake. They're the ones who insisted. They're the ones who threatened me into taking the job. I know how we're supposed to tremble when you look in our direction, I know how easy and how often you cook the evidence to suit your whims, but I'm not going to payoff on a lousy job like this."

"I KNOW who will payoff," he said. He tried to bully me with his eyes. "The Strickland reps have already approached me, and about half the rest of the people in your department, trying to get something on you. They'll pay plenty for this."

"Sell it," I answered instantly. "Don't pass up your big chance, man. Meantime, I'll ask the Starmen if it makes any difference to them whether I'm a Doctor or a Mister. If they don't want me as their go-between you've got yourself a big deal. But if they do want me—well, I don't know if you'd noticed, but I saw what they could do to their enemies."

His eyes were no longer cold and bargaining. He fled.

That left, of the central corps, only Sara to bully me about not making any appointments with the Starmen—a job any secretary ought to be able to do. Certainly the world's foremost authority on Extraterrestrial Psychology ought to be able...

"Awright, Sara!" I finally snapped back. "Stop nagging. We're not married yet, you know!"

Her eyes grew big.

Come to think of it, I guess that's something else I hadn't thought to take care of when I should.

CHAPTER EIGHTEEN

I MIGHT stand on the smear slide and shake my fist in resentment at the eye looking down through the microscope at us, but it had no apparent effect on the biologists who were stirring up our environment to test the potentials of our reaction.

The next exasperating move of the Starmen was reported on the television set in my office. I'd left the thing turned on because even my brief visit with them had given me another perspective. Now I was looking at the antics of the human race as they might appear to a detached, alien mind in curious observation.

Out of nowhere the star sapphire globe suddenly appeared again, this time over the street in front of Blair House. There was panic pressure in the crowds of people directly beneath it, but the perimeter crowds were pressing inward to get closer this time. They could not move out of its path of descent.

I watched in apprehension mixed with some sardonic satisfaction. This time the Starmen, those lovable boys, Bex, Dex, Jex, Kex and Lex, must reveal that the globe was an unsubstantial illusion, or they must crush the people beneath and violate their own precepts of not harming another life form.

They solved their dilemma, but not mine, by performing another miracle. I might have known they'd not hesitate to impress the yokels with their magic.

They came through the doorway of Blair House, again dressed in their resplendent uniforms, again with those irrepressible boyish grins on their handsome faces. They grouped together there at the entrance. The crowd fell silent. The leader, I suppose it was Bex, spoke familiarly with the crowd.

"Folks," he said, and without seeming strain his voice reached the outermost limits of the crowd, "I reckon we oughta clear up a little mistake we made. The other day that recording we played said we was here as ambassadors. Well, shucks, we're not. I guess, back on our world, ambassador means something different from here. We didn't know we'd be insultin' anybody by not meetin' with all the ambassadors from all your countries.

"And we're not in any position to make any deals with anybody about anything. So that's why we asked Mr. Kennedy not to put us down for talks with all you people of importance."

(They came in lies and deceit. They hadn't asked me any such thing. The matter hadn't even come up. Still, I breathed a sigh of relief.)

"You might say," Bex continued to sell his winsome personality. "Instead of being ambassadors, we're more like—well, tourists. We don't want to disappoint nobody, but that's kinda what we'd like to do a little more of.

"We're gonna tour around now, to see a little more of this beautiful world of yours; that is, if you don't mind. We figger we oughta see the country a little before we go back home. Maybe we can figger out how to give you a helping hand here and there. You might say we're a kind of Youth Peace Corps—in a small way, that is.

"We want to thank you for the nice reception and the nice parties you gave us yesterday, but we hope it won't hurt no body's feelin's if we hafta turn down any more invitations. We're not used to all this celebratin', we're just plain fightin' men.

"You keep in touch with Mr. Ralph Kennedy at the Pentagon about us, he's a mighty fine fella, and we certainly appreciate all the valuable time he's given us. We'll keep in touch with him too, long as we're visitin' here on your fine world.

"We'll be back before we hafta go home. So long, now."

A RAINBOW suddenly sprang out of the side of the hovering globe and placed its end at their feet. They marched up the rainbow and entered a hatch, which opened at their approach. The blue glow from within the ship was cut off as the hatch closed again.

And there was no ship there.

Some claimed stoutly that they were able to follow its incredible speed up into the heavens, some confused specks before their eyes with the dot of the globe disappearing into the blue.

I had an idea it was something else; some movement perfectly

"A rainbow suddenly sprang out of the side of the hovering globe and placed its end at their feet. They marched up the rainbow and entered a hatch which opened at their approach."

normal to the experimenting biologist, inconceivable to the germs on the smear slide. But why bother to explain themselves to the germs? To keep the environment as "natural" as possible, within controlled conditions, changing only those things they wished to alter?

Personally, I wished they'd make up their minds. What were they? Ambassadors, tourists, fightin' men, Youth Peace Corpsmen? Each role required a different response from us, each label carried its own set of expected behaviors.

This was a question I felt Dr. Gerald Gaffey and his phalanx of semanticists might wish to ponder. He and I had grown friendlier since that first meeting, and when I walked into his office this time, I was a little surprised that the original icy hauteur was back. The two scientists with him, both of international renown, looked at me with open hostility. Then I realized.

Twice the Starmen had referred to me in this latest speech of theirs, and both times as Mister. I was a Mister who had been posing as a Doctor. I was beneath contempt. Nothing was said, of course. Nothing needed be.

I had made up my mind to tell them, before they went out on the limb too far in the speculations of these Good and Evil Galaxial Civilizations, that they'd better also take into consideration that the whole thing had been a staged illusion. I changed my mind now. I knew from experience that anything a layman might say could not possibly be credited.

And, anyway, what difference would it make to the biologist what one germ on the smear slide thought of another?

"Never mind," I told him, and walked out without mentioning why I had interrupted their important conference in the first place.

WE heard nothing from the Starmen, or no reports of their whereabouts, for two days. This didn't mean we heard nothing about them. There was page after page, hour after hour of hash and rehash.

The newest miracle of Walking on a Rainbow stirred and disturbed us even more than the balcony scene that first night at Blair House.

Now, for the first time, we took public note that in the battle between the Globes and Discs there had been no debris to fall upon us. It was another miracle.

That the discs had almost won, then suddenly turned coward and fled was a miracle.

That our tracking equipment and scientific instruments generally had failed to work, failed to confirm what our eyes and noses, our ears and tactile senses had told us was real—this was a miracle.

"First thing you know," I said sourly to Sara, "We'll be like the mountain Indians of Latin America. A tourist drives through a village at the breakneck speed of fifteen miles an hour and doesn't kill anybody. It is a miracle. The sun shines through a rift in the clouds and lights up a mariposa lily on the hillside. It is a miracle. A man wakes up in the morning, after he has dreamed he was dead. He is alive. It is a miracle."

She looked at me without committing herself.

"Accept as basic premise that by individual whim we can suspend the natural law of the entire universe, and anything you want to name becomes a miracle." I said.

"What natural law would you use to walk on a rainbow?" she asked me.

"Now, Sara," I chided. "That's like saying, 'If you're so smart why ain't you rich?'. Hell, I don't know all the natural laws there are. Nobody on Earth does. Maybe the Starmen know some natural laws we don't know, and maybe they don't know all there are either. But that doesn't mean because we don't know the natural law, there isn't one."

"So you believe in natural laws you don't understand, and others believe in miracles they don't understand—and what's the difference?"

"We can never understand the miracle. Someday we can understand the natural law. That's the difference."

"The miracle is easier," she said lightly. "Think of all the scientific study you have to do to understand natural law."

"Oh, Sara," I groaned. "You, too?"

"So what kick do you get out of being such a cynic?" she asked. "If we want miracles, what's wrong with miracles?"

I started to answer with the old bromide, "Only the broken hearted idealist can become a cynic," but it sounded too corny and too complicated.

IN two days, a new series of miracles began.

The biologists began to mess up the culture they were studying in earnest. First news came from Western United States. From Austin, Texas, to the barren shores of the Pacific in Baja California, and upward to the badlands of the Dakotas and on upward into Canada, subterranean streams of water geysered to the surface overnight. The water was as fresh as that from mountain springs. It was seeping into the desert lands, flowing through the arroyos, forming lakes in box canyons, forming its own interwoven network of irrigation ditches. Within weeks the entire desert would be green with growing plants. Within a year, it would become rich farmland.

Let the Agriculture Department groan about its already too expensive surplus crops. It was a miracle.

Only the lag in communications, caused by lines clogged with diplomatic recriminations for our hogging the Starmen all to ourselves and trying to extend Yankee Imperialism to the entire universe, prevented us from knowing at once that the desert regions all over the Earth were receiving like treatment.

News came from the Sahara region next, then the Arabian Desert, the parched plains of India, then the Gobi. Australia was furious for being treated as if she were down under until suddenly her whole interior became a network of canals, streams and lakes.

Brazil was in the act of complaining that just because she had no deserts was no reason why she should be deprived of her share of miracles when word came that the vast Amazon region had been penetrated with networks of clearings and highways to checkerboard her many thousands of square miles of jungle. Almost in the manner of mycelium growth, the clearings spread up into Central America and momentarily stopped those people from shaking angry fists toward the North and South. Interior Africa and the jungles of Southern Asia next reported.

Russia was reaching new heights of bad manners until she noticed that the snows of Siberia were melting to release more millions of square miles where more comrade workers could refuse to grow enough grain to feed the toiling masses who had little personal incentive to toil. Greenland, Canada and the State of Alaska hardly had time to draft protests before the same phenomena caused them to tear up the drafts.

There was a week of this. Hardly more than enough time for the land speculators to recast their investment programs to cash in on these profitable miracles. Hardly time for people to start packing their goods for the biggest land rush in all history—hardly time for governments to pass laws telling the people they couldn't do it, not until the land investors had got set for profit taking. Hardly time for Russia to wonder where she would send her variant thinkers now that Siberia was a potential paradise. Hardly more than time for us in the Pentagon to do more than keep statistics on authenticated and rumored miracles.

IF Economists expressed alarm over the disruption of normal trade, if Scientists expressed alarm at the potential ocean level rise because of all these melting snows, nobody heeded. Economists are about as accurate as weather forecasters or horse race handicappers, and who pays any attention to scientists when there are miracles?

United States did find time to do a little muttering in Uncle Sam's beard. Figured on an area for area basis, certain other countries were receiving more miracles per square miles than we; and was that fair? Of course we were still ahead on a per capita basis—and so how you looked at it depended on whether you wanted to complain or brag.

Yes, indeed, the Starmen were varying the chemistry of the culture on the smear slide.

I looked at these changes with dread. They were so vast, with consequences beyond imagining—while man can tolerate only the smallest of change at anyone time.

…It took a thousand years, fifteen hundred years, of placing the holy image exactly in the center of the canvas before man could tolerate the blasphemy of placing it slightly to one side.

…For seventeen hundred years Ptolemy's astronomic system of placing the Earth at the center of the universe satisfied the vanity of man, including his astronomers, before the courage of Copernicus to say it might not be so. And five hundred years after Copernicus, in the scientifically enlightened year of 1958, one third of American high school students still believed the Earth to be at the center of the universe.

...Change one word on the label of a product, and although they cannot read it, five hundred million Chinese will refuse to buy it. How ignorant can those natives be? But—

...Oh yes, we once tried to put this thick catsup in a wide mouth bottle so it would pour easily, and the company almost went broke—the American housewife refused to touch it because the shape of the container had been changed. It has taken us fifteen years to enlarge the neck of the bottle by one quarter of an inch. And—

...It takes ten years to change the lapel line of men's suits.

...Oh yes, we like to see fresh, new ideas and treatment in stories, but we can print only those exactly like those we have printed in the past.

...A popular song must be written in exactly thirty-two measures. State the theme in eight. Repeat it in the second eight. Bridge with another eight. Repeat the theme for the final eight. Otherwise a musician cannot play it, the people cannot learn to sing it.

...A man may take one step ahead of his culture and chance being called a genius. But if he takes two steps, he is certain to be called a menace, a madman, a fool.

...The humanist does not make even one step ahead, and thereby maintains his secure control of men's minds. No one knows, or cares, how the scientist thinks, so long as he continues to make things easier without really changing anything. So he may say, "If my theory doesn't work it must be wrong, and I must recast my notions about the true nature of this until I find a theory which will work." If he gets any kick out of confounding himself with all this self doubt, he's welcome to it so long as he doesn't disturb the certainties of the rest of us. But the humanist says, "I cannot be wrong. If my theory doesn't work someone else is at fault and must be punished." In all man's history there has been taken not one single step forward from this attitude among the humanists.

And so I looked at these changes caused by the Starman, and dreaded.

I SHOULD have known better. Past experience with a quarter

million individuals should have taught me. I should have known that a man can receive only what his mind has been prepared to receive, that all else is ignored, or interpreted to suit his prior interpretation—that man can only accept change through it being interpreted as no change, or not knowing it is change.

Apparently I needed a reminder. Sara brought it into my office in the form of sample mail we were receiving—mail addressed to the Starmen, routed through us.

Our department's mailroom had done an excellent job of classifying the letters according to type. There were some forty six thousand letters and telegrams represented by the following:

"My corn patch is gittin purty dry. Rain on it. Yrs trule."

There were only four thousand, five hundred antonym letters in this category:

"Urgent you not let it rain on Ladies Aid picnic for worthy cause."

A few hundred said something like:

"Have twenty dollars with bookie on a longshot, Sea War, in the second. 50/50 split with you if you make him win."

Some six thousand pleaded with them to use brand products in their next personal appearances, or came within the following patterns:

"Enclosed find eleven genuine simulated gold embossed lifetime passes to any theatre showing our pictures. Usual requirement that you give your independent, unbiased opinion that picture is stupendous, collossal, gigantic applies. Lifetime passes absolutely guaranteed good for ninety days. Cancellable without notice."

"Request you furnish our department store chain with one gross real live Santa Clauses for coming Christmas season. Must have real ones. Kids are wise to phonies, pull off their beards and kick them in shins for not keeping last year

promises. Causes much union grievance. For your information, enclosed is traditional editorial telling why belief in Santa Claus is necessary—and which says nothing at all about how sales would drop off, factories shut down, and newspaper (which carries the editorial) advertising space cut down without said belief. Absolutely necessary our citizens be kept believing there is a Santa Claus. As twig is bent tree will grow. Fight communism. Send us real Santa Clauses. We pay union scale."

UNFORTUNATELY, statistics on the following kind of letter were incomplete since loyal mail clerks had been tearing them up before it was realized we should keep an impartial check:

"Toiling masses greet their comrades from space. Party requires you make unmistakable statement against grasping capitalists within next twenty-four hours. No excuses, or you know what."

But there were one hundred and twenty four thousand letters of the following kind:

"Eyes of blue, five feet two,
Bette Lou, and she's pretty too. That's just a little rime the boys made up to teese me with, and I guess it does tell you what I'm like, but it didn't make me stuck up, not a bit. I don't think if a girl is inteligunt and beautiful, crushingly divistatinglly beautiful she doesn't need to be stuck up. Do You? Anyway I'm not, not a bit, stuck up I mean.
"I feel it is my sacred duty to write you and tell you what the nice girls in my town are saying about you..."

I LOOKED up from reading the letters. "People," I commented unhappily. "Whether it's some kind of science we don't understand, yet, or miracles we'll never understand, it doesn't change a thing. I thought it was really going to bollux up the works, but it doesn't. Before the Starmen, people looked to science for miracles. They didn't know how the scientist got them, they didn't want to know, they didn't listen when he tried to tell them. All they wanted was the miracle, not a lot of instruction, which would be work to understand. Well, now they've got the miracles from another source, without any instruction on how to go and do likewise. But there's no real difference, no real change from then to now."

"I guess people will go right on being people," Sara agreed, as if that would comfort me.

APPARENTLY Shirley, and Dr. Gaffey, and Dr. Kibbie had also been busy, behind the scenes, working for my comfort.

The three of them walked into the office, at that moment, without appointment. The two men had broad, happy grins for me, and file folders of papers in their right hands. Shirley's beautiful, old homely face was wreathed in misty smiles. She carried a file folder in her right hand, and a big dry-goods box in under her left arm.

As ranking seniority in my department, she stepped forward first.

"Galaxy Admiral Kennedy," she said solemnly. "I present you with the document making you Galaxy Admiral." She opened the file folder, laid it on my desk, and surely enough, there were the words, the signatures, the seal. "Those publicity seeking—uh—people down in Space Navy wanted to be in on the presentation, but I convinced them you'd want it kept in the family, first, before all the hoopla of television, newsreel, and the rest of it. I hope that was right, Galaxy Admiral, Sir."

"That was exactly right, Shirley," I managed to gasp.

Then she laid the big dry goods box on the desk top, and whisked off the lid. I saw the midnight blue of textile within the box, and a gleam of brass and braid. Much brass and braid.

"Your uniform," she said proudly. "I thought you'd want it right away."

I looked down at my white shirt, which had been fresh this morning when I put it on, but wasn't now. I looked down at my faded slacks which, eons ago, had been pressed.

"I suppose that's part of the penalty of being a Galaxy Admiral," I said, and already felt a twinge of nostalgia for the good old civilian days. "I hope it fits."

"Oh it will fit," she answered confidently. "I made N-462 give me your exact measurements."

I opened my eyes wide at that calm statement.

"You knew?" I asked.

"Sure, I knew he was a cop," she said. "But it was better to have him where I could keep an eye on him than to let him run loose. In his own way, he was doing his job. He had all your measurements down to the last quarter inch."

"I hope not all of them, Shirley," I said solemnly.

The old gal blushed, and for the first time since I'd known her, she broke into a rumbling roar of laughter. "You kill me," she chuckled.

DR. Gerald Gaffey, standing behind her, and next in line, gave a loud "Harrumph!" then stepped forward. He, too, flipped open a file folder and laid it on the desk.

"Doctor Ralph Kennedy," he said solemnly. "Here is your PhD in Extraterrestrial Psychology."

I looked at the name of the famous university, and the signatures at the bottom of the scroll. It was no purchased quickie that I need ever be ashamed of.

"How is this possible?" I asked. "It doesn't merely say 'Honorary'."

"In view of your contact with the Extraterrestrials," he murmured. "The only Terrestrial who has had private conferences with the Extraterrestrials..."

"I'm glad," I said simply. "There've been some things I've wanted to tell you. And now I can, now that I'm in the union."

Dr. Kibbie then stepped over and laid his gift on the desk.

"Another two billion," he crowed happily. "A special committee, with special war emergency powers..."

"Good God," I said. "I haven't finished spending the last two billion, yet."

MR. Harvey Strickland was unhappy.

He sat in his purple robe in his Washington office, and pawed sourly at the late edition newspapers on his desk. The editors were following his instructions to the letter. There were paeans of praise, gratitude for all this foreign aid and good deeds from Youth Peace Corpsmen (which would enrich the fortunate and impoverish the unfortunate even more), the clear interpretation of the divine nature of the Starmen, the bead strings of blessings, the exhortations to his millions of readers, who bought their daily ration of ready cooked opinion from him each day, to get down on their knees and grovel in the dust.

But it was not enough.

Everybody was being too damned glad about it all.

There wasn't...there wasn't anybody to hate. That was the missing element. No villain anywhere.

It was all right to crusade for something, provided it is a milksop something safe and popular, like home and flag and mother; but nothing really starts to happen until you come out against something. And that's got to be a personalized something, somebody you can get your teeth into. You can be against sin, but there's no real fun in it until you've gone out and located yourself some sinners.

And what's the point of being for something, unless you can grab up the torch, the knife, or the bullwhip to use on someone who isn't also for it? The way you bring about the disintegration of a community or a culture is to turn loose the self-righteous with no holds barred. But how can you have the full enjoyment of self-righteousness unless there's somebody to persecute?

What were the lines from that obscure writer of thirty-forty years ago? Oh yes...

Hide! Hide! Witch!
The good folk come to burn thee,
Their keen enjoyment hid beneath
The gothic mask of duty.

And there wasn't a single witch in sight. But there must be a witch in the underbrush somewhere. There had to be. There was always somebody you could make out a witch. Dammit, everything was brought up to a peak; the fervor was running in full flood, and not a smell of anybody to pull the bloodhounds baying, to call forth the robes and light the torches.

The damn Starmen were being too impartial with their favors for everybody. That was all wrong. It wasn't done that way. You always favored somebody at the expense of somebody else. Then to keep the bloodhounds from attacking the favored, you always found a false scent to pull them clear away from the scene. That was the way it was done, the human way.

You give the humans some witches to burn if you don't want 'em to notice what's happening.

THERE was only one human who had had more than the most casual social contact with the Starmen. And that one was damn near untouchable. He had been made a Galaxy Admiral, and Harvey Strickland hadn't been able to block it. He had been made a PhD, and even there the Strickland threats of cutting off all future donations to that university had arrived too late to stall the act. He'd been given another two billion dollars to spend, and the damn congressmen had just laughed and said, "Well, Harvey, you ought to be able to figure out some way to get your cut of it—as usual."

His mounting fury at one Dr. Ralph Kennedy congested his veins to turn his face purple.

There ought to be a way. There had to be a way.

And what the hell had he been thinking of? Of course there was a way. He was a newspaper man, wasn't he? And wasn't the first thing a cub reporter learned on his first interview the way? You threw away what the guy actually said. You made up the things you wanted him to say, and put them in quotes. You hung these on just enough of the truth to make them believable.

His tensions relaxed, and he began to smile. No underling could be trusted with this one. He would go to see Galaxy Admiral Dr. Ralph Kennedy, in person. So let the stupe deny, scream denial. Who'd print it? Who ever does?

He snapped his fingers to bring Miller to him, to fetch his clothes, to help him dress, to accompany him to the Pentagon. In the contortions of dressing, his hand happened to brush against the left side of the loose jacket Miller was wearing today. He touched the gun through the cloth, the gun too amateurishly worn in its shoulder holster.

He froze for an instant, with his mind racing through the possibilities. He excused himself to go to the bathroom. Miller was not needed in this task. This was a demand he had been saving against the day when Miller might show a reviving spark of pride; this to be the final degradation of the once proud and haughty most popular man on the campus.

FROM a concealed space in back of the medicine cabinet he drew forth an elaborate bulletproof vest. He had no trouble, all by himself, in stripping to the waist, putting on the vest, dressing himself again. With all his mountainous rolls of fat, an added inch of girth would never be noticed. He had no fear for his head. The amateur murderer, handling a gun for the first time, always shot at the biggest part of the target.

The things you learn in the newspaper game! You never know what might come in handy.

His high, wheezing laughter was still wreathing his face in a grin when he came out of the bathroom.

The smile froze on his face.

The fax machines were chattering like monkeys gone crazy. Miller had the TV monitor turned on and was staring at it incredulously. But there was no mistaking the news. As fast as one bulletin cleared, another came through.

"Bulletin…Santa Fe…New rivers and lakes in the desert have suddenly disappeared…Jet aircraft shot aloft reports entire horizon empty of water… Other areas confirming entire Southwest desert dried up…dust storms howling…early sprouting seeds blackening…land investors ruined…

"Wait a minute…another flash coming in…the warm air in Canada, Alaska, turned to howling blizzard…many surveying parties representing land investors believed trapped…no word yet from Siberia…no…here it is…same thing in Siberia…Moscow threatens reprisals against United States for harboring Starmen…

"Another bulletin…Rio…the Amazon jungle has closed in again…no more clearings and highways…

One after another the bulletins poured in, the cancellations of the good deeds of Youth Peace Corpsmen—true human behavior, once the enthusiasm had worn thin, the publicity had been milked, let loose, let the whole thing disintegrate.

He wondered if the Starmen were all that human; that they could shrug it off with, "Well, we came and showed you the benefits you could have. It's not our fault if you failed to pick up and maintain what we gave you. We did our part."

A slow smile began to stretch his lips.

What the hell. It didn't matter what the Starmen were thinking or doing now. Once the shock of loosing all these goodies had worn off, the whole human race would be screaming for blood, somebody's blood, anybody's blood. The whole human race, which he so despised...

And he had the power of opinion making in his hand...

He looked at Miller, standing there in front of him, meek, licked, powerless, smouldering down underneath perhaps, but helpless. Planning violent revenge for what had been done to him, but doomed to failure. The whole human race was a Miller, his Miller.

The grin broadened into a grimace of pure glee.

THE cancellation bulletins were still pouring in over my own TV monitor, when Sara came in from her buffer office. Her eyes were wide, her face was pale, her lips were taut.

"What does it mean, Ralph?" she asked in a low voice.

I shrugged helplessly.

"I think the biologists have finished running their experiment with the culture," I said, with a wry smile. "I think they're getting ready to go home, and are tidying up the lab to leave it in the same state they found it."

"You never did believe they were for us," she said.

"Nor against us, either," I answered. "Why should they be? How long is the human race going on believing it is something so damned special that the universe and everything in it has to be arranged to suit man's convenience?"

"Maybe you're right," she said. "What I came in to tell you is that there's a Mr. Harvey Strickland and his secretary waiting in my office to see you. I don't know how they got past all the security checks, but they're here."

"It's taken him longer to get around to me than I expected," I said. "Maybe he's been waiting for the right moment."

"He's picked a good one," she agreed.

She correctly interpreted my nod of assent, and stepped back to open the door. The two men must have been standing there on the other side of it. The fat man's face was already clouding with anger at the les majesty of keeping him waiting.

"Mr. Strickland, Mr. Miller," Sara murmured as they came through the door. "Galaxy Admiral Dr. Ralph Kennedy," she introduced me unnecessarily.

"Find this gentleman the widest chair we have, Sara," I said soberly and in a tone of utmost courtesy.

She had been my secretary for years. Not one line of her face altered, but I noticed there was a new lightness to her step and less dejection in her shoulders as she stepped over to a huge overstuffed, and murmured, "I believe the gentleman will find this comfortable." Sara was exploding with perfectly concealed laughter. The world had not come to an end, after all; not really.

She touched another chair for Miller, but he ignored her. His face was pale, his breathing harsh, his forehead beaded with sweat, his hands at his side were trembling. His eyes were riveted on Strickland, and Strickland alone. Neither the chair, nor the room, nor the rest of us existed for him. He remained standing, a little to the side, a little behind his boss, as a good organization man must.

WHEN Strickland had wheezed and eased himself into the depths of the chair, I sat down too, and folded my hands on top of the desk. Sara was looking at me inquiringly.

"I doubt that the true record would ever find its way into the popular press or on TV channels, Sara," I said drily. "But stay and take notes, anyway."

Strickland's head jerked at that. He looked at me piercingly from out the rolls of fat around his eyes, and the slow grin appeared on his face.

"This is going to be a pleasure," he rumbled. "Another young squirt who thinks he's lord of the Earth."

"I've managed somehow to keep my head up, and my backbone straight," I said modestly. I deliberately looked at Miller, and felt my words penetrate that rapt preoccupation. His own head seemed to come up a trifle, his own back seemed to straighten. His right hand started to raise, then lowered again.

"I don't know why you've endured the nuisance of coming

here," I said to Strickland. I was using moderate tones, words slowly spaced. I knew this man for what he was; I'd been around Washington long enough now and enough people had become sufficiently confident of me to talk to me. I'd met other men like him, congressmen and senators who believed their districts and their states to be their own private hunting grounds, and the people in them their political serfs and game. Most of these had no other motive except self-preservation; the corrupting years had given them assurance they were of superior clay, their behavior simply to see that none challenged that truth. Mr. Harvey Strickland was driven by compulsions running deeper than Lord of the Manor keeping his serfs under control.

"You already know what you're going to report out of this meeting," I continued. "You're looking for a patsy, and you've found one. You know, as well as I, that I have no power and no influence with the Starmen, whatever. If you've got any sense at all, and you've got plenty, you know that they've been fiddling around with the environment of this life form they've discovered; and what I might think about it makes no more difference to them than what some germ thinks about the chemical changes some biologist makes in the culture medium on a smear slide."

His grin grew wider. It was my only answer.

"The mob is going to be howling for blood," I said. "They're always ready to blame somebody, and you'll get your kicks out of giving them somebody. It would never occur to you to use your power and your influence to build men, to build intelligence, willingness to think, willingness to shoulder responsibility for their own mistakes, to help them grow up. Because if they did that, you might not be such a hot specimen. And that's the realization you can never face."

He threw back his head and roared with laughter.

"I'll bet you were the most popular man on the campus," he said, between high, wheezing gasps.

THAT was one thing he shouldn't have said. Miller jerked like a marionette on agitated strings. His right hand swept up under his unbuttoned jacket; he pulled out the small gun; he pumped shots at the body of the huge man; one, two, three, four, five, six.

There was the thud of each, the flinching of the flesh, the slight sway to one side at the force of repeated impact—and the high, wheezing laughter.

Miller's eyes widened, his jaw dropped. Now he was trembling violently. He stared at the laughing man in horror, the full surge of his belief in Strickland's invincibility returned. His knees crumpled. He sank to the floor there in the middle of the office. He cradled his head in his arms braced by his knees, and sobbed in loud, wracking coughs.

I had half risen, bracing my hands on desk top. Sara was sitting still and frozen. I could understand, I, too, was frozen in that crouch before a leap around the desk to stop him. Strickland was calmly unbuttoning his shirt, and searching in the mesh of his bulletproof vest for the slugs of lead. As he found one, he would lift it between thumb and forefinger, hold it up as one looks at a pebble specimen, then lay it carefully on the smoking stand at the side of his chair. He was collecting a little pile of them. I was sure he would find them useful in the future.

I settled back down in my chair and began to breathe again. I did not punch any of the buttons under the front rim of my desktop. There was no emergency. And I doubted that the spat, spat, spat of the gun had been heard outside the office. Oddly, I heard myself still talking in measured tones, and this time to Miller huddled there on the floor.

"It wouldn't have solved anything," I was saying. "There's always been Stricklands around. There'll always be Stricklands around until people get tired of swallowing ready-made opinions and slogans like cure all pills. This Strickland was only one of the series, and it wouldn't take long to replace him with another. Personally, I think the people deserve him."

Strickland looked up from his preoccupation with his little pile of misshapen bullets. He stared long at me from the creased rolls of flesh.

"I could use a man like you," he said as if making an important discovery. "By God if I couldn't!"

"But by God you won't," I said.

"You know the score," he went on, as if I hadn't spoken. As if the matter were already arranged. "Now this is the next step we'll take…"

His voice trailed off, and his own eyes widened. I hadn't believed it possible to see so much of them. His own face went slack, and the flesh suddenly sagged. The whole body seemed to slump and overflow the edges of the chair. The head dropped suddenly, as far as fat would allow, toward the chest.

And only then did I become aware that a purple vortice was whirling beside my desk.

I seemed to be past shock, past caring. Perhaps I had been expecting them, preparing for their coming, ready for any kind of form in which they might appear.

"Bex, Dex, Jex, Kex and—ah—Lex," I said drily. "I think you've given the man a heart attack. Granted that one was long overdue with all that fat around it. Is this how you go about carrying out your resolution to harm no one?"

MILLER still cradled his head in his arms, his face concealed. He had not yet seen the vortice. Sara was still huddled back in her chair, staring at the purple whirlwind.

"It's all right, Sara," I said. "These are our little playmates who just like to have fun. I think this is probably how they really look. All the other he-man stuff was just showmanship. More illusion. You know, same as people?"

She nodded, but out of habit only. I wouldn't have been surprised to see her fingers transcribing it all in shorthand, without the faintest notion of what I was saying.

"Still," I said to the vortice, "it might be a little chummier if you did take human shapes." I nodded toward the slumped figure of Miller, who hadn't yet looked up.

They obliged me. Five handsome, splendid young men were standing about the room. At the stir, Miller did look up then.

"Your boss is dead," I said.

His face stiffened, and then he smiled.

He held out his hands, wrists together, toward the nearest Starman.

"They're not policemen," I said. "Sara, take him down to first aid. Let the Strickland body be until I see what these slaphappy fly-boys want now."

As if she, too, were a puppet on a string, Sara arose, reached out to Miller, helped him pull himself to his feet, helped him out the door. As they went across the room I wasn't sure who was leaning on whom.

"Well?" I asked, when Sara had closed the door behind them. I nodded toward the Strickland body again.

I do not know, to this day, whether the Starmen felt emotions in the way we feel them. They portrayed emotions, and I suppose any life form must have emotions of some kind. Wouldn't it be a part of awareness, awareness of self, awareness of self in relation to things about us, awareness that things, even though unpersonal and impersonal, can harm or benefit us according to our use of them? These Starmen had at least the courtesy, if nothing else, to look regretful.

"Your criticism of our mistakes is nothing compared to what Galaxy Council will say," Bex said.

"I thought you told me yours was a policy of noninterference, of bringing harm to no life form," I said.

"We have restored everything to its original state."

"Oh no," I answered. "You've been here. You've made yourself known. If nothing else, nothing else at all, we'd never be the same again."

"That's the point," he said. "You will be the same. Because the Vegans were here, thousands of years ago. Prematurely, without authorization. You've built up an entire structure of thought based on their appearance. In time, our appearance will come to be just more of the same."

"But we were progressing out of it," I said. "Our belief in demons was fading. Compared with what you can do, perhaps we hadn't made much progress in science, but we were starting off in that direction. Now you've set us back at least a thousand years."

"We miscalculated," he said, and had the grace to look unhappy about it.

"You sure did," I agreed fervently.

"It's still difficult to believe that you've made the advances in nuclear physics, other quite commendable advances in other fields…"

"Thanks," I interrupted drily.

"And still know nothing, nothing at all about yourselves. We miscalculated. We believed there must be two life forms. We didn't see how a man could master science in one area of knowledge and be as ignorant and superstitious as a savage in another. We believed that for some reason the intelligent race must be in hiding. We didn't then know that this intelligence was being hidden, not only from his own kind, but from himself.

"Otherwise we wouldn't have made an appearance at all."

"And having made the appearance… But if you were courting an intelligence, why the guise of—well—such hero types?"

"We felt there must be some desperate reason why the intelligence was concealed. We fitted the mores of the lesser form, lest our appearance lead to revealment unwittingly."

"SO now," I said, "You've made your tests and done your exploring, and you've found that while we can mix together a little of this and that and make a big bang, emotionally and philosophically we're still ignorant savages. That we've made a little progress in the physical sciences, but in the humanic sciences we are still determined not to make any progress. I suppose you'll—uh—ah— quarantine us? See to it that we don't get out beyond our solar system?"

"Oh no!" The reply was instant, and shocked. "We wouldn't have any right to do that. Who are we to say how a life form shall develop? When you get out there, if you do, if your humanists permit your science to develop any farther and that's unlikely, we'll cope with you somehow."

"Our humanists may fool you," I said. "You hadn't noticed, because it is such a tiny trace; but here and there we even have a humanist who is willing to admit that his authoritative personal opinion and vested importance as a leader not ever to be challenged might not, after all, be the whole and final answer."

I nodded toward Strickland's body.

"That guy's an amateur compared to some of the humanists we've had and what they've done to the human race. But don't count on us failing. That would be another miscalculation."

THE star sapphire globe, iridescent from pearl to blue, hovered once more in the center of Washington's Mall. Once more the sad eyes of the Lincoln statue looked out upon it.

The crowd was thinner now, and quiet. The dignitaries were few. Men, such as the President, had calculated the political disadvantages of appearing too intimate with these Starmen who had given of miracles, and taken them away. No one, this time, seemed eager to challenge my position as go-between, host speeding the departing guests upon their way.

There were a few officers from the Pentagon, bless 'em, who had shown up; as if to say, right or wrong, the services will stand behind their own. The crowds of the curious had gathered, but they were neither enthusiastic nor hostile. The death of Strickland had left a hole, a deep hole not yet healed, and no one had yet turned public opinion toward the Starmen into hate. Lacking leadership in forming slogans, for this temporary space, the news media were simply reporting events. It was something new for this generation, and no one knew how to respond to it.

We stood, a little lonely group; the five Starmen somehow less resplendent this morning under a clouded sky, Sara and I, Shirley and Dr. Kibbie and Dr. Gaffey, a handful of lesser Pentagon officers.

We stood by the ramp (no rainbow bridge this time) and gravely shook hands with the five Starmen. They turned and filed up the ramp. There were no cheers from the crowd.

Four of them filed into the blue radiance shining from the interior, an interior our scientists had never got to explore. The fifth, I suppose it was Bex, turned and faced the silent people. So he was going to carry out my plan of saving face, after all!

"People of Earth," he said, and his voice came clearly to all of us. "I reckon you all are disappointed that we hafta go home now. But like your own Peace Corps we came, and we showed you how to turn wasteland into bountiful fertile acres. We done our duty by you, and I reckon now that you know what ought to be done, you'll go right ahead and do it. We showed you. We done our part."

He waited.

There was no answering cheer.

"Goodbye now. When you all have figgered out how to sail across space to our shores, you'll find yourselves just as welcome as the people who come to your shores."

There was a murmur from one of the officers behind me.

"Why the dirty, hostile sons-of-bitches!" he said.

Bex turned then, and walked into the blue radiance. The ramp slid, melted into the side of the ship. The door closed. The globe lifted; slowly at first, then faster and faster.

It melted into the layer of clouds. It was gone.

The silent crowd shuffled a little, and slowly began to disperse.

THEY had come from the stars, and Earth would start its long road to recovery.

I looked at Sara, Shirley, Gaffey, Kibbee.

"Well, boys and girls," I said. "We're still the Bureau of Extra-terrestrial Psychology. Maybe some of the obscure research departments of some of the universities will still want some information from us."

"We may have to hoard that two billion and stretch it out for quite a while," Dr. Kibbee answered.

The three of them turned then, and started walking toward our staff cars, ahead of Sara and me.

"I wonder if Old Stone Face might hire back a couple of wandering personnel people," I mused.

Sara grabbed me by the arm and halted me. She spoke intensely.

"Look, boss," she said firmly. "Everybody's shocked now. After that they're going to be mad. They'll be as mad as hornets for a while. And then they're going to start thinking. Now that we know that outside our solar system, now that we know it is there; how long do you think it's going to be before we grit our teeth, dig in, and determine to go out there, ourselves? Come hell or high water!"

Shirley, Gaffey, Kibbee had stopped when we did, and now they drifted back.

"Why sure," Kibbee began to bubble again. "And that two billion will be just a drop in the bucket compared to the money we can promote for that kind of program."

"Doctor Kennedy, I'm going to need much more scientific help than I've got if I'm to carry my share," Gaffey said, and began to look far away into a dream.

"And, Admiral," Shirley said, "I think we ought to use this lull to get reorganized for the big push."

"Okay, kids," I said. "You're right. We're not licked. We're just starting."

The Space Cadet chauffeurs saw us turn and start walking briskly toward them. Even at that distance they began to catch the sudden enthusiasm our strides and faces revealed. They straightened up, pulled their space helmets into ready, climbed jauntily into the cockpits of the automobiles, and when we had slammed the ports behind us, they blasted off down Pennsylvania Avenue.

THE END

If you've enjoyed this book, you will not want to miss these terrific titles…

ARMCHAIR SCI-FI & HORROR DOUBLE NOVELS, $12.95 each

D-11   **PERIL OF THE STARMEN** by Kris Neville
  THE STRANGE INVASION by Murray Leinster

D-12   **THE STAR LORD** by Boyd Ellanby
  CAPTIVES OF THE FLAME by Samuel R. Delany

D-13   **MEN OF THE MORNING STAR** by Edmond Hamilton
  PLANET FOR PLUNDER by Hal Clement and Sam Merwin, Jr.

D-14   **ICE CITY OF THE GORGON** by Chester S. Geier and Richard Shaver
  WHEN THE WORLD TOTTERED by Lester del Rey

D-15   **WORLDS WITHOUT END** by Clifford D. Simak
  THE LAVENDER VINE OF DEATH by Don Wilcox

D-16   **SHADOW ON THE MOON** by Joe Gibson
  ARMAGEDDON EARTH by Geoff St. Reynard

D-17   **THE GIRL WHO LOVED DEATH** by Paul W. Fairman
  SLAVE PLANET by Laurence M. Janifer

D-18   **SECOND CHANCE** by J. F. Bone
  MISSION TO A DISTANT STAR by Frank Belknap Long

D-19   **THE SYNDIC** by C. M. Kornbluth
  FLIGHT TO FOREVER by Poul Anderson

D-20   **SOMEWHERE I'LL FIND YOU** by Milton Lesser
  THE TIME ARMADA by Fox B. Holden

ARMCHAIR SCIENCE FICTION CLASSICS, $12.95 each

C-4   **CORPUS EARTHLING**
  by Louis Charbonneau

C-5   **THE TIME DISSOLVER**
  by Jerry Sohl

C-6   **WEST OF THE SUN**
  by Edgar Pangborn

ARMCHAIR SCI-FI & HORROR GEMS SERIES, $12.95 each

G-1   **SCIENCE FICTION GEMS, Vol. One**
  Isaac Asimov and others

G-2   **HORROR GEMS, Vol. One**
  Carl Jacobi and others

If you've enjoyed this book, you will not want to miss these terrific titles...

ARMCHAIR SCI-FI & HORROR DOUBLE NOVELS, $12.95 each

D-21   **EMPIRE OF EVIL** by Robert Arnette
          THE SIGN OF THE TIGER by Alan E. Nourse & J. A. Meyer

D-22   **OPERATION SQUARE PEG** by Frank Belknap Long
          ENCHANTRESS OF VENUS by Leigh Brackett

D-23   **THE LIFE WATCH** by Lester del Rey
          CREATURES OF THE ABYSS by Murray Leinster

D-24   **LEGION OF LAZARUS** by Edmond Hamilton
          STAR HUNTER by Andre Norton

D-25   **EMPIRE OF WOMEN** by John Fletcher
          ONE OF OUR CITIES IS MISSING by Irving Cox

D-26   **THE WRONG SIDE OF PARADISE** by Raymond F. Jones
          THE INVOLUNTARY IMMORTALS by Rog Phillips

D-27   **EARTH QUARTER** by Damon Knight
          ENVOY TO NEW WORLDS by Keith Laumer

D-28   **SLAVES TO THE METAL HORDE** by Milton Lesser
          HUNTERS OUT OF TIME by Joseph E. Kelleam

D-29   **RX JUPITER SAVE US** by Ward Moore
          BEWARE THE USURPERS by Geoff St. Reynard

D-30   **SECRET OF THE SERPENT** by Don Wilcox
          CRUSADE ACROSS THE VOID by Dwight V. Swain

ARMCHAIR SCIENCE FICTION CLASSICS, $12.95 each

C-7   **THE SHAVER MYSTERY, Book One**
         by Richard S. Shaver

C-8   **THE SHAVER MYSTERY, Book Two**
         by Richard S. Shaver

C-9   **MURDER IN SPACE** by David V. Reed
         by David V. Reed

ARMCHAIR MASTERS OF SCIENCE FICTION SERIES, $16.95 each

M-3   **MASTERS OF SCIENCE FICTION, Vol. Three**
         Robert Sheckley, "The Perfect Woman" and other tales

M-4   **MASTERS OF SCIENCE FICTION, Vol. Four**
         Mack Reynolds, "Stowaway" and other tales

www.ingramcontent.com/pod-product-compliance
Lightning Source LLC
Chambersburg PA
CBHW030310180626
46810CB00003B/1006